The Fate of Farringale

Modern Magick 12

Charlotte E. English

1

AT HOME IN YORKSHIRE (or Derbyshire, one is never so impolitic as to specify), spring is, at last, springing, and deliciously. I don't know whether House is celebrating something, but there are early roses everywhere, and most of them are pink. The air smells like heaven; I've taken to leaving my bedroom window open all the time, though it's only April. It's warm enough.

Over the course of the winter, two possibilities have emerged:

Either the voices behind the wallpaper are holding an interminable greengrocer's market, or—

I am, at last, going quite mad.

If I sit, as I often do, on the floor in some out-of-the-way corner of the House, with my face pressed inelegantly to the wall and my eyes closed, I can *hear*....something. *Rhubarb rhubarb rhubarb,* says somebody. Several some-bodies.

I mentioned this to Jay, once or twice (which was brave, wasn't it? If anyone is going to imagine me stark raving bonkers I'd rather, above all, that it wasn't Jay). He didn't seem appalled so much as... tired. 'Oh?' said he, mildly enough. 'Is this to be the beginning of another whirlwind magickal adventure?'

I don't know that he was ecstatic at the prospect, which is fair enough. It isn't so long since I contrived to drag him into a dance-off with a horde of the unquiet undead, and a man doesn't get over a thing like that in a hurry. 'I don't know,' I answered, honestly enough. 'They really do seem to be talking about comestibles.'

'Comestibles,' Jay echoed. 'There are voices in the walls and they're talking about provender.'

He said this with a certain flatness in his tone, and a hint of the wary side-eye. Bad signs. 'Rhubarb, mostly,' I hastened to assure him. 'Nothing *particularly* bizarre.'

'Very reassuring,' agreed Jay. 'No one has ever launched a bloody rebellion over fruits and vegetables, but confec-tionery, now. That would be a different matter entirely.'

I nodded enthusiastically. 'Who among us hasn't at least thought about it, occasionally? Let's overthrow the government and install the Pastry Queen.'

'Armies of ladyfingers and eclairs,' Jay concurred. 'Brutally efficient, and really rather sweet about it.'

'No, but really,' I persevered. 'That *is* what it sounds like.'

Jay attempted no further remonstrance. I suppose, given everything that has occurred of late, the notion that there are voices chatting behind the wallpaper and they're partial to summer fruits isn't particularly strange. 'Let me know if there's any mention of cucumbers,' he said, wandering off. '*Then* we should definitely be concerned.'

There hasn't been, that I've been able to discern. Just the rhubarb.

The thing is that I've learned how to listen, and I mean *really* listen. It's part of being the new Merlin. Even rocks have something to say for themselves, if you can catch the trick of their language. Houses, now: houses have a *lot* going on.

And our beloved House is a positive hive of industry and conversation, if only I could catch the trick of *that* language. I can't, quite, and I'm convinced House is doing it on purpose.

I began this morning in fruitless (so to speak) communion with the ladies and gentleman behind the wallpaper, as I too often do; parked, this time, in the first-floor common room, cross-legged upon the floor by the window and with my face pressed to the wainscot.

Rhubarb rhubarb, whispered someone.

The fine folk of the Society have ceased to question me on this behaviour, which can only mean I am developing a reputation for such eccentricity there is no further use in even trying to understand me. I can't say that I mind. Where's the fun in being the living embodiment of Albion's most ancient magick if you can't be battier than a belfry at Halloween?

Today's adventures *progressed*, shall we say. The process of deep-listening to the land (as Ophelia, previous caretaker of Merlin's magick, would have it), is delightfully mindful: I sit and breathe and listen and absorb until I am *one* with the world around me. Not quite literally, although sometimes *very* literally, and in this case—

Rhubarb rhubarb, the voices uttered, tantalisingly just beyond the range of clear hearing, and I pressed my face closer to the wall with eyes closed and mind very much on another plane of reality; listened to our beloved House in its every feature: the gentle *creak* of its timbers, the wordless steadiness of its stones; the warm, spring breeze wafting through its open windows; the rattle and clatter of its occupants, busily engaged with the nothings and some-things of the day. I felt myself sinking, by slow degrees, melding my consciousness with that of the House until I could almost have been one of those voices behind the wallpaper; I could *almost* reach them, *almost* distinguish real, whole verbiage—there were words in the midst of the garble—I had only to stretch a fraction farther and I'd have it—

A sense of sudden pressure assailed me, fracturing my concentration. A *weight*, resting heavily upon me, stop-ping my breath: I twitched, and then *heaved*.

The pressure lifted; somebody uttered a surprised sylla-ble.

Then I heard my name.

'Ves!' said the somebody, and as my consciousness sep-arated from the House and drifted slowly back into its rightful spot I realised that it was Jay. 'Ves, is that you? What the—'

I stretched, or tried to. My limbs did not cooperate; seemed, in fact, to be warped into some unfamiliar con-figuration; I shook myself mightily.

Jay thumped my head, or what had taken the place of my head: it came to me, dimly, that I had developed up-holstery.

'Ves,' Jay said again, impatient now. 'This is ridiculous, even for you.' Rather irritable, for Jay: I detected in the irascible words a strong note of concern.

'To be fair,' I uttered, manifesting vocal chords from somewhere, 'this isn't as bad as it could have been.' I referred, of course, to a prior escapade, in which I had turned myself (inadvertently, I hasten to add) into a large rock; a Fairy Stone, to be precise; an object so impervious to human interference that I might, were I unlucky, have remained in said shape eternally.

'Come out of that,' Jay said severely. 'Or I'll be forced to sit on you again.'

'You wouldn't!'

'You're an exquisitely comfortable armchair.'

I felt obscurely pleased by this tribute. 'Exquisitely! No, am I really?'

'The living replica of my own, very favourite chair, except for the general purpleness of you. A discrepancy I might have noticed sooner, were I not very absorbed in this treatise on Yllanfalen architecture.'

Ooh. 'I want to read that,' I said, instantly.

'It's just arrived. Your mother sent it over.' Jay, curse him, was smug.

My mother—being the current queen of an ancient Yllanfalen kingdom (don't ask)—has access to all sorts of delicious intellectual goodies, though I usually have to twist her arm rather hard before she'll share them.

Of course, if I wanted to read *anything* ever again, I'd have to stop being a chair first.

'Jay,' I said in a small voice.

'Yes.'

'I think I'm stuck.'

'Do you want me to fetch Zareen?'

I never did learn exactly what Zar had done to me, on the occasion of the Fairy Stone debacle. I only knew that it had hurt, even when I was a slab of rock. 'No,' I said hastily. 'I can do this.'

Jay waited. He did a creditable job of appearing coolly unconcerned by my plight, like a man whose confidence in my capacity to get myself *out* of the absurd fixes I get myself *into* can only be described as "boundless". But I can detect an aura of supreme, if suppressed, tension from a hundred paces, even as a chair.

'I'll be all right,' I told him.

'I'd be glad if you could demonstrate that in more tangible fashion. Fairly soon.'

'Is that Jay-speak for "I'd like to hug you so tight you can't breathe?"'

'I might crack a rib. Possibly two.'

An enticing prospect. Hm.

If I'd thought myself into an involuntary oneness with the House, surely I could think myself into a voluntary restoration of Self. I could start with that purpleness Jay had mentioned, my favourite colour; the moment I was Ves again I'd switch my hair to something vivaciously violet. I thought about cuddling Goodie, the unipup; the soft, velvet feel of Adeline's gorgeously equine nose; my best dress, and – of course – the relatively new, but perfectly delightful sensation of being wrapped in the arms of Jay.

And when that didn't work, I went on to hot chocolate – the kind Milady served in silver pots, if she was pleased with me; to stacks of pancakes with ice cream; to laughing with Jay over some trifling joke, and the thunderous expression on Val's face if she thought I might have dog-eared a page in one of her precious tomes (and I would *never*).

'Jay,' I said, in an even smaller voice. 'I really am stuck.'

'Okay,' he said, with forced calm. 'Wait one moment, I'll get help—'

I didn't have time to prevent him from dashing away (*don't leave me*, the small, frightened part of my soul pleaded). I was kicked; not physically but psychically, somehow; as though some obliging, never to be enough revered personage had delivered a swift *clout* to the insides of my brain; and there, I had eyeballs again, and hands, and limbs with which to cling (a little shamefully) to Jay.

'What happened,' said he against my hair.

I attempted a breath, and achieved a slight one; he hadn't been joking about the cracked ribs, quite. 'I think—I think House helped me,' I managed; and at the back of my mind, as though uttered from a great distance away, came the immortal words: *Rhubarb, rhubarb.*

Thank you, I responded, and added, for good measure: *strawberry, strawberry.*

'This Merlin thing,' said Jay, without in the slightest degree loosening his grip on me. 'Are you sure you're getting it right? I mean, legend says he was capable of shape-shifting, but he tended to choose useful things, like birds. Never heard anything about chairs.'

A fair question.

All the inherited wealth that is Merlin's ancestral magick was now mine entirely (until I chose to retire, and pass it on). Ophelia had deemed me ready a month or so prior—or perhaps she had simply grown weary of carrying it all around herself; it is no inconsiderable burden.

I wasn't ready, of course. We'd both known that. But no one's ever ready, not really; not for the thorny, meaty, complex challenges of life. One merely throws oneself in, and manages, somehow—or hovers on the bank for eternity, never quite mustering up the nerve to step off.

I was managing, sort of. And I still had Tuesdays with Ophelia; I'd ask her about the Chair Debacle next time—

My train of thought ended there, for Jay had gone tense again—was positively rigid with it, it was like cuddling an ironing board—'What's the matter?' I prompted.

'There's a—' He stopped.

I poked him in the ribs: no response.

I tried, then, to withdraw myself from the circle of his arms, but that proving ineffectual, I turned us both about, so I was facing the window, and he had his back to it.

A familiar, placid scene met my searching gaze: the prismatic green lawn that is House's pride and joy stretching away to a horizon clustered with old oaks, one or two of my esteemed Society colleagues strolling about upon it; those roses, roses everywhere, in a thousand shades of pink and peach; the vast, fathomless expanse of the sky soaring above, lightly streaked with wafts of drifting cloud—

And a shape there, a shadow, a distant winged form coming closer—

Jay released me and spun, visibly shaking himself. 'Sorry,' he said. 'It's odd, but for a minute there I thought I saw—'

'Griffin,' I croaked.

'Yes, I thought I saw a griffin, but that can't possibly be...'

We fell into a mutual silence, for the dark little silhouette bombed over our beloved old oaks and shot towards the lawns: and there could be no mistaking it, as the seconds passed, no mistaking it at all. We had seen these before, these glorious, majestic beings, the kings and queens of mythical creatures, in undisputed possession of lost Farringale; had declined absolutely to tangle with them, unless *obliged*; and now here—here came one of them, at *speed*.

2

JAY AND I STAYED frozen like that a moment longer—and then *ran*, full tilt, down the corridors and stairways to the ground floor—to the nearest of the many side-doors—I reached it first, hurled it open, pelted out onto the lawn, breathless and staring. A few others were spilling out of the House around me, and the griffin, when it came to land, had an audience of adepts readying Wands and spells and hexes—

'Wait!' I shouted, half involuntarily, hardly knowing what I was saying, but—

'Ves, are you crazy?' That was Marian, readying a devastating blast of something aimed to kill, or at least maim, and she was good, she'd hurt it for certain—

'Don't,' I pleaded. 'Just give it a moment.' I'd seen griffins when they were intent on destruction and this didn't look at all like that. There wasn't nearly enough lightning.

'She's right,' said Jay from right behind me. 'I don't think we're in danger.'

The griffin loomed right over us by then, unthinkably huge; a long shadow fell, the sun momentarily hidden behind enormous, feathered wings.

'You're both crazy,' Marian opined, and I could see her point: if the griffin had attacked us from such a vantage point we'd all have been dead in seconds.

It didn't. Its desperate speed slowed; it drifted lazily down, wafted like dandelion seed, until its great, taloned feet connected with the rich green grass—

Light flashed—

I blinked rapidly, my eyes streaming—and when the blindness faded and I could see again, the griffin had gone.

Before us, statuesque, and making a grand, sweeping curtsey of effortless elegance: a lady of unmistakeable troll heritage, and a great, grand lady at that.

I knew her. I'd seen her before.

'Baroness Tremayne? Surely not—it can't be—'

Jay said: 'Wait, Baroness Tremayne? The one you met in Farringale—'

'Yes.' I returned the lady's curtsey; she isn't so much old-fashioned as *old*, impossibly so, survived somehow since the days before Farringale's fall, and she's an aristocrat. One shows respect.

She nodded to me, and to Jay, her gaze sweeping unseeingly over the crowd assembled around us. She looked: harried. Her white hair formed a dishevelled halo around her troubled face, and her gown, as handsome and rich as ever, was soiled with cobwebs and grime.

I'd never quite seen her in the flesh before; not like this. She lived—or existed—a step outside of time; "between the echoes", she called it, a hazy, indistinct state that preserved her indefinitely. A lonely existence: she watched over Farringale, had done so down the long ages since its fall.

Previously I would have said *nothing* could have brought her out of Farringale.

Now: only the very direst emergency could have done so.

A stab of profound unease unfurled within.

She spoke, her voice rusty with disuse. 'I must—I bring dire news. I must see Mab.'

She hadn't come all this way looking for me, then. I smothered a twinge of disappointment. 'Mab?' I echoed. 'I don't think we know anyone by that name—'

She interrupted me; the heights of rudeness in so grave, so courteous, a woman, but she could not wait for me to finish my trailing, unhelpful syllables. 'She is here. I know her to be. I must see her.'

'I—' I began, and stopped, for at that moment my phone, tucked into a pocket in my dress, began to buzz. Not an unusual occurrence, but a feeling of foreboding swept over me, and I hurriedly fished it out.

An ornate, silver chocolate pot dominated the screen: Milady calling. As Jay interrogated the baroness about the identity of "Mab" (assisted, or impeded, by numerous interpolations from others), I stepped away to answer the call. 'Milady?'

'Ves,' she said crisply. 'We have a problem.'

'It seems so,' I agreed. 'Although this particular griffin isn't a danger to us—'

'Griffin?' Milady uttered the word sharply, with a *snap*: unmistakeably a question.

'You... you aren't calling me about the griffin?'

'I am calling about Silvessen,' Milady said. 'You will have to explain to me what you mean about the—'

'I'm coming up,' I said, shamelessly interrupting in my turn.

'Quickly,' Milady agreed, and hung up.

I grabbed Jay's elbow. 'This morning grows ever more interesting,' I informed him. 'Baroness? I believe you should come with us.'

HOUSE TOOK PITY ON the ancient baroness—or perhaps its attendant colony of obliging fruit-fanciers had grasped the sheer urgency of our various missions;. Either way, we entered the House via a side-door and emerged, with a single step, into Milady's tower-top chamber. A plump arm-chair materialised almost immediately, and I assisted the baroness into it: she, winded and weak, sank into its comfortable embrace with a sigh. Her eyes closed, briefly: when they opened again, she said, 'Ah, Mab.'

The air sparkled frenetically. 'Who is—I don't quite—Ves, enlighten me.'

Having never before encountered anything but a perfectly self-possessed Milady, I could only gape; my uneasy feelings deepened into a yawning crater of alarm.

It was Jay who said: 'Milady, this is the Baroness Tremayne, of Farringale. Baroness, Milady is the leader of our Society. Whatever has occurred at Farringale, I am sure she will be able to assist—'

'Morgan,' said Milady. 'Ves, you never mentioned the baroness was also Morgan le Fay—'

'I didn't *know*,' I put in, distressed.

At the same time, Baroness Tremayne said, again, 'Mab. I did not know these were emissaries of yours.'

Jay said, 'You mean *Milady*—'

'What's happened with Silvessen?' I interjected, my head whirling.

'The regulators are gone,' Milady said, clearly, into a sudden silence.

'From Silvessen?' I said, recovering my wits. 'The regulators are *gone* from Silvessen?'

I hadn't had occasion to visit Silvessen for a few weeks, but when I'd last been there, everything had been progressing beautifully. Our artisans (including my father) had rebuilt large parts of the village; a small but enthusiastic population of Yllanfalen were moving in, most of them from my mother's kingdom; and the regulators were doing a resoundingly good job of restoring and balancing the magickal flow in Silvessen Dell.

My head began to whirl again. 'You mean they've—they're faulty, or—'

'I mean that someone has taken them,' said Milady.

Someone had dug out the regulators from Silvessen Dell—and, just as that news reached us, so had Baroness Tremayne.

Surely, not a coincidence.

Jay and I, silent with consternation, looked at the baroness, and waited.

'Farringale is no longer inviolate,' Baroness Tremayne told us. 'There has been—an incursion.'

'Who,' I said, faintly.

'I hardly know,' said the baroness—Morgan, as she also was—that explained her griffin shape, legends claimed Morgan le Fay could take the form of any animal, and surely that would include the magickal ones—my brain was spinning; I forced it to focus.

Milady had been silent, absolutely silent. At last she spoke: 'These things cannot be unconnected.'

My thoughts exactly. 'Baroness, did these intruders bring devices with them—they are made from argent, highly potent things—'

'I do not know what it is they have done, but it has—the disruption is—severe. The city stands in sore need of aid.'

I could well imagine what kind of disruption might afflict Farringale, if someone had taken Silvessen's regulators there.

Well, scratch that: I *couldn't* imagine it, nobody could. We had tested the devices in a town where magick was, had been, dead; drained away down the ages, its Dell dormant and inert. We hadn't yet tested what the regulators could do, *would* do, in a place like Farringale: potent still, disordered, chaotic. Dangerous.

Ideally, they would help restore balance: the lost city would be calmed, settled, by them. But if that had been the case, would Baroness Tremayne have come here, desperately seeking help? No.

Besides, there had been only two regulators installed at Silvessen: nobody knew, no one could guess, how many might be required in so gravely disordered a place as Farringale. More than two, anyway.

A question circled in my gut, sickening me with foreboding: I had to ask it. 'When you speak of an "incursion", Baroness. Just...how many people do you mean?'

'I hardly know,' she said again. 'You must understand. It is—chaos.'

I did understand. Farringale was subject to great surges of magick; when such chaos as that held sway, there could be no maintaining any sound grip on reality whatsoever.

'Have you an estimate?' said Milady. 'I must have some idea of the extent of the problem before I can decide how best to help.'

'They are...' Baroness Tremayne shook her head. 'They seemed to be everywhere.'

My hopes, feeble as they were, lay in pieces. She wasn't talking about the kind of minor *incursion* I had made into Farringale, once or twice in the past; just me and a few others poking at things and taking notes. This was on another scale.

She wasn't talking about an incursion so much as—as an invasion.

'Giddy gods,' I breathed. 'This is some kind of *war*.'

'I do not know what their goal may be,' answered the Baroness. 'I did not show myself to them—yet.'

She had got straight out in search of help, and had come to us.

Well, who else could she go to? The Troll Court couldn't intervene; the ortherex infesting half of that city were supremely dangerous to them.

Wait, though. She hadn't come to ask the Society for help.

She'd come to ask *Mab* for help.

A living archetype herself, when faced with an unanswerable threat, she had fled to another—the only other, perhaps, that she knew.

Milady.

'I'll help,' I blurted. 'I mean, I'm only a new Merlin, but there must be something I could do—'

'Ves,' said Milady.

'Yes ma'am.'

She was quiet for a moment. Jay and I, and possibly Baroness Tremayne, sat in breathless silence, awaiting her decision.

'We will, of course, assist in every way we can,' she decreed. 'But first we must understand what we are up against. Ves.'

'Yes ma'am!'

'And Jay. As two of the very few who have set foot in Farringale at all, I will be requiring you to conduct reconnaissance.'

'Anything,' I said.

'It appears that this assignment may be dangerous, so you will be taking Rob with you.'

Jay seemed about to speak, but Milady forestalled him: '*Not* Indira. Not yet. I would like you to go unseen by these interlopers, if you can, and I am therefore inclined to limit this assignment to the three of you. Ves, any special assistance you are able to offer as Merlin will be fully necessary.'

In other words, I had a *carte blanche*.

'I will requisition the appropriate keys from Mandridore immediately. You will leave as soon as they arrive.'

Which begged an interesting question: how had these interlopers got in? There was only one known way into Farringale at present, and it took three separate keys, one of which *we* held. If that were missing, Milady would have known about it already.

One of the several questions we would have to find answers to, and quickly.

'Baroness,' said Milady. 'Will your state of health permit you to—'

'I shall return with your representatives,' said Baroness Tremayne, firmly.

'That would be ideal,' said Milady, with palpable approval. 'Rest assured they will attend to your safety.'

'And I, to theirs,' answered she, with just cause. She was Morgan le Fay: what strange and ancient arts might she have at her disposal?

'Please, prepare yourselves,' concluded Milady. 'And quickly. You may requisition anything you require from Stores.'

Meeting adjourned. Jay and I filed out in a tense silence, leaving the Baroness to confer with Milady further.

Outside, I stopped, momentarily overwhelmed.

Someone had plundered our prized new tech from Silvessen, Farringale was under some kind of attack, and Milady turned out to be the living embodiment of a faerie queen.

'Shit,' I observed.

Jay said, 'Verily.'

3

I KNOW THIS MAY seem hard to believe but I am actually the very soul of discretion, most of the time.

Not that my new status as the current Merlin is a secret, exactly. But I haven't broadcast it to the far corners of the earth (or, at least, the Society), and neither have my nearest and dearest. I'd like to hang on to my identity, I suppose: I'm Ves, most of all.

That being so, I had no intention of instantly spreading the news of Milady's secret identity all through the House (or Baroness Tremayne's, either). In fact, I was incredibly restrained; I told absolutely no one at all.

Well: no one except for Val, anyway. Sort of.

ALERT, read the text I sent her the second I was at liberty. *Code reddest of RED: urgent information requisition. What have you got on Morgan le Fay and Queen Mab?*

Note that I didn't say why I was asking. I felt quite proud of myself.

OH! Came Val's response. *Been wondering about that for the LONGEST time.*

SUSPICIONS CONFIRMED.

Stand by: information overload incoming.

I didn't ask her which suspicions, or to whom they pertained. I didn't dare.

So much for subtlety.

Morgan le Fay. Said to be one of the most powerful enchantresses in British history. Connections to the supposed King Arthur, etc. Unlike the aforementioned probably did exist in some form—known archetype but hasn't been heard of in ages and I mean literal ages, Ves.

Trust Val to text in words of several syllables.

Known or at least reputed powers: shape-shifting, especially into animal forms. Also illusions, famously castles-in-the-air or like mirages.

I filed those thoughts away: maybe there'd be something we could use.

Mab: info sparse, Val went on. *Famously mentioned in Shakespeare; facility with dreams implied; once monarch of a now defunct faerie kingdom.*

Mention in same bracket with Morgan suggests subjects related?? Never heard of Mab as an archetype but could be. Would explain a lot.

I hastily wrote back. *I don't know what you mean nothing is explained I'm explaining nothing.*

Lol, said Val, most uncharacteristically. I took this unusual utterance to be expressive of profound sarcasm.

Nothing to see here, move along, I returned, and put my phone away before I could compromise myself—or Milady—any further.

I'm practiced at packing light and packing fast, and these days—to Ornelle's relief—I don't tend to need much from Stores. I was ready to go in under an hour, buzzing with energy and alarm, and with nothing to do but wait for go time.

I went out to the Glade.

I don't know if you've ever tried it, but nothing soothes the spirit like a tranquil hour or two in a magickal grove littered with unicorns. Extra points for being One with the Horn Squad yourself. I was feeling rattled when I came in, head all awhirl, nerves on highest alert; not the ideal state in which to undertake a top secret mission of the greatest importance. I needed the prismatic calm of a mountain lake, especially if I was going to have to go in there and Merlin all over the place. People expect more from the living embodiment of the most famous wizard in Britain than they do from a mere, common-or-garden Ves (including me).

An hour or so of sweet, juicy grass, dulcet spring sunshine, and (inevitably) fragrant roses and I more or less had it. Serene, smooth waters, fathomlessly blue. Doves cooing peacefully as rose-stained dawn breaks over a softly rippling meadow. The unearthly tones of panpipes at—

'VES!'

My head shot up, several half-chewed stems of grass falling out of my gaping jaw. That was—that was *not* Jay, that was another male voice, a familiar one—I was off at a gallop before I'd even finished the thought, and so much for the mountain lake.

Baron Alban stood at the mouth of my sacred glade, inflating his lungs in preparation for another earth-shattering bellow. I ran at him full-tilt and planted my nose into his massive chest, almost knocking him over (and with a person of Alban's stature this is no mean feat).

'Oof,' declared he, grabbing my face. He planted a smacking kiss on my nose, and glowered at me: a confusing combination. 'I'm here to deliver a key,' he informed me as

I went questing through the pockets of his jacket (I could smell baked goods somewhere in there, I swear). 'Which means I'm here to dispatch you on a mission of probable danger and I can't go with you.'

Alban had been part of our first, only minorly disastrous mission to Farringale. It could have been catastrophic: Alban could have fallen prey to the ortherex, the malignant creatures infesting the depths of Farringale (and several other Troll enclaves). They were deadly; they'd have eaten Alban alive, if we had been unlucky.

We wouldn't—*couldn't*—risk that again.

'I wish you could come with us, too,' I informed him, though little of it emerged past my equine teeth.

Alban patted my neck. 'I would understand you better if you were Ves-shaped. Just saying.'

I felt a curious reluctance to step out of my glade, my sanctuary. Once I did, I was committed—off to Farringale, and whatever fresh disaster awaited us there. Off to wield some of the most ancient and powerful magick in the country, in one of the most ancient and powerful magickal courts in the country, and try desperately not to mess it all up.

Courage, Ves.

I took a deep, whinnying breath, and stepped over the invisible threshold of the glade. The moment I did so, the transformation began: within a few shuddering, uncomfortable seconds I was myself again, with arms as well as legs, and fabulous hair.

The hug I immediately received was, I felt, recompense enough. It was *engulfing*.

'Mmf,' I said against Alban's grey silk shirt.

'Sorry.' He eased the pressure of his massive arms, and I could breathe again.

'It may sound shockingly ungrateful,' I told him, 'but I wish just a little bit that I'd got Morgan's magick rather than Merlin's. The Baroness showed up as a *griffin*, Alban. A griffin! And flashed out of it again easy as pie. Imagine that.'

'Ves, two minutes ago you were an actual unicorn. Four legs, horn, everything.'

'I know. Exactly. That only happens when I step into the glade, and fades again as soon as I step out. And I'm only ever a unicorn. I have no control over it.' I indulged myself in a few moments of green-eyed envy, picturing myself soaring over the land upon the wings of a creature of legend.

'Surely you've accomplished something equally marvellous as Merlin?' said Alban, proving himself as superb a diplomat as ever.

'This morning I turned myself into a chair,' I concurred. 'That's not nothing.'

'A chair.' Alban twinkled at me, wordlessly.

'I didn't mean to,' I admitted. 'I haven't really got the hang of this Merlin thing.' Merlin's magick seemed to be of the land: the magick of tree and stone, of air and water, and the vastness of it appalled me almost as much as the poeticism of it enchanted me. I probably needed a solid decade of practice before I could call myself a creditable Merlin—if then.

'You'll be marvellous,' Alban replied, apparently reading my thoughts.

I put away my anxious face, replacing it with a set expression of firm resolve. 'Marvellous or not, I've got to go.'

He nodded, and dug a hand into a pocket in his trousers. The keys, when he handed them to me, were blissfully cool against my hot fingers: thoughts of that serene lake returned. They were gold and bronze, exquisitely worked, and set with rubies and emeralds: the fanciest of fancy. Typical of the Troll Court. 'I half expected to hear they'd been stolen,' I told Alban, tracing a finger over a glimmering ruby.

'I don't know how these intruders got into Farringale, but it wasn't with the keys,' Alban confirmed.

I sighed, and carefully vanished the keys into an air-pocket: Indira's trick. It'd taken me much longer to master it than I liked to admit, and I might never have been able to do it at all without Merlin's magick. 'I'll take the best care of them,' I said.

'And of yourself, too, please.'

I nodded. 'Always. All right, here I go.' I dropped a hasty kiss on Alban's cheek, flashed a beaming, confident smile, and took off at a run for the House.

JAY AND ROB WERE already waiting for me. I found the pair of them in the cellar, pacing in circles around the Way-henge House keeps for our resident Waymaster's particular use. Jay displayed a key for me the moment I stepped in: wrought silver and gleaming sapphire-blue: the third key we needed to open the gate into Farringale, the one House has in its keeping.

'I've got the other two,' I told him. 'Alban just brought them.'

Jay nodded. He was tense and terse, barely speaking: I was oddly reassured to learn that it wasn't just me feeling the pressure.

Rob, though, smiled at me. I was even more reassured by his presence, and it's partly because he's a big, visibly capable man, the exact sort you'd like to have around if there's trouble in the offing. But he's also the collected type, radiating calm and cool, and I breathed a little easier in consequence. 'All set?' he asked me.

I patted my satchel. It wasn't as burstingly full as it used to be, my need for paraphernalia being somewhat diminished. But it held an article of supreme importance: Gallimaufry, or Mauf, our semi-sentient encyclopaedia of everything. We had acquired the book from Farringale in the first place (or its predecessor: Mauf was a clever copy). I didn't know for sure that we would need his extraordinary reserves of knowledge, but it never hurts to have a know-it-all along, now does it? 'I've got two magickal keys and one remarkably well-mannered tome,' I informed Rob. 'All set.'

'Then we're going,' said Jay, in a tone one doesn't argue with. But he squeezed my fingers when I took his hand, a note of affection I very much welcomed.

'Wait, we're forgetting Baroness Tremayne,' I pointed out.

Jay shook his head. 'She's already gone back. Griffin shape. She's waiting for us.'

Right. Great. I stayed quiet as he mustered the Winds of the Ways: he's well practiced at it by now, but it seems a delicate process. A strong breeze circled about the henge, tossing my hair; the world began to turn around me; I shut my eyes.

A vast, slightly sickening *whoosh*, and we were gone.

4

AN ODD FEELING, RETRACING the steps of our first (and at the time, secret) mission to Farringale. We were almost the same company again, missing only Alban; the journey through the Ways was the same, bringing us out on the same sun-dappled hilltop near Winchester. Even the season was the same: had it really been a year ago? A whole year! And yet, only a year. We might be the same team on the same mission, but we were not the same people.

I wasn't the same Ves.

Nor was this mission conducted in the same exploratory spirit as before. Where previously I had felt excitement, curiosity, a twinge of guilt (see: aforementioned secret status), now we were tense and focused, prepared to encounter a very different Farringale. I scarcely noticed the vivid yellow-flowered shrubs, or the shimmering blue bowl of the sky. I went straight for my syrinx pipes, played a distracted melody thereupon: down came Adeline, for me and Jay to ride, and her larger, darker friend for Rob.

Jay, once rendered almost prostrate by the effort of carrying three or four people through the Ways, stood superbly composed and in control: not even the prospect of a horseback ride through the skies had the power to unsettle him now. How far we've come, I thought, with an odd twist of pride; a feeling I had no time to indulge or to share, for we were in a hurry. I paused only to touch noses with Addie before I mounted up, and Jay scrambled up behind me. Rob took the lead, a godlike figure enthroned upon stallion-back: I spared momentary wisp of pity for whoever had been so unwise as to mount a foray in Farringale. They were going to regret it.

Ten miles or so winged away in no time at all; ten miles of crisp, clear air, Addie's velvet hide shimmering in the sunlight, and Jay a warm, comforting weight against my back.

Then we were spiralling down and down, alighting near Alresford, at the bridge over the River Alre. How sturdy, how dependable a construct, this thing of dark bricks and weathered stones: staunchly guarding the entrance to

Farringale for hundreds of years, immoveable by time or mischief; untouched, and untouchable—

These high-blown musings upon time and change came to an abrupt end as Addie planted her four silvery hooves upon solid ground, and I got a closer look at the agèd bridge.

Not so untouchable after all, and not untouched. It's the type of bridge that looks like half a small castle: built from pale grey stone in great, heavy blocks, with a handsome pointed arch spanning the river beneath. It's been there for eight hundred years, probably, and you'd think nothing could touch it, but something *had*.

That majestic arch lay shattered in several pieces, each one as large as my entire body. The back half of the bridge had crumbled, fallen in, lay blocking the river; water was forming a new path around the obstacle, split into a streaming fork. It was as though the hand of some kind of god had smashed it in a fit of pique: a single, stunning blow, and an irreplaceable piece of architectural history lay in ruins.

I stared at the devastation, too numb with shock to think, let alone speak. 'Who—' I began, but words failed me. I felt a tear spill down one cheek; more in anger than grief, though surely some of both.

Who could have committed an act of such wanton destruction? Who could have so little respect for history, for heritage, for art—

I'd forgotten Farringale, for a moment. I was recalled to duty by Rob's grim pronouncement: 'Well. We know how they got in.'

'What?' I looked up, away from the tumbled mess of stone and time. 'But—just destroying the bridge shouldn't open the gate, surely. It should make it inaccessible.'

'I know it *should*,' Rob agreed. 'But it hasn't.'

I saw what he meant. A nimbus of light hung somewhere under the remains of the bridge, a light I recognised: we'd passed through it before. On the other side lay Farringale.

Whatever they had done, it hadn't been a physical act of destruction. The bridge had been wrecked by magick, and whoever had done it had hacked the gate open by the same means. A vicious, brutal, graceless stroke, committed by one whose only goal was to get inside, and hang the consequences.

Jay was already on his phone, talking in crisp, short sentences to someone from the Society. '—completely wrecked—gate's clearly accessible—seriously urgent—'

I stepped nearer to the destroyed gate, my stomach flipping with alarm. Baroness Tremayne had talked of many intruders, too many to count, but hearing about it at some distance was one thing: seeing the evidence of this savage incursion was quite another. This was an invasion indeed, the destroyed bridge the kind of collateral damage inflicted by a hostile army.

'Shit,' I whispered, my head spinning. Farringale was in *deep* trouble.

Rob had been quiet for some minutes. At last he said: 'This is much more serious than we anticipated. I'm half inclined to abort mission. Come back with greater numbers.'

I saw his point. We were woefully overmatched. But on the other hand—

'We aren't here to try to remove these people, yet,' I reminded him. 'We're here to get a clear picture of the situation, so we can counter them more effectively later. What are we going to tell Milady, if we walk away now? We've learned almost nothing.'

'Ves, there are three of us. *Three*, against—' He waved a hand illustratively at the destroyed bridge, unable to specify precisely what the three of us faced.

And it was that very vagueness that worried me. 'We've got to learn more,' I argued. 'Who are these people? What do they want with Farringale? Giddy gods, how did they get past the griffins? If we're to have the slightest hope of besting them then we've got to answer these questions.'

Rob gave me one of his grim looks. I don't mind admitting that it is a little intimidating. 'And how do you propose we proceed? We'll be spotted as soon as we step through that portal.'

'Not necessarily.'

Rob stared at me, waiting. Unimpressed.

'Did I never tell you how I first met Baroness Tremayne?'

'Not in any great detail, no.'

'She was—she doesn't exist in the real world, precisely.' I held up a hand as he made to object. 'Yes, I know she *does*; we saw her, not long ago. But she's ancient, Rob. She's hundreds of years old. She's survived by existing outside of our reality, for the most part. She calls it *between the echoes*. I was in there with her, for a bit. It's like—you can't be seen by anyone outside of it, not even if you're standing right next to them. She can pull us in, she's done it before, and we can sneak around as much as we need to.'

A light of interest dawned in Rob's dark eyes, and I knew I had him. 'Are you sure?' he said, ever the health and safety manager. 'There's no danger?'

'There's probably some,' I admitted. 'But not *much*.'

Rob's mouth twitched in a smile, mostly suppressed. 'Right,' he said.

'It's too much to hope for *no* danger. I mean, when was the last time that happened?'

He answered with a shrug, or perhaps he was merely rolling his powerful shoulders, preparing for action.

Jay appeared at my elbow. 'They're sending some people to have a look at the bridge situation,' he informed us.

'We can't wait for them,' I said. 'There's no time to be lost. Who knows what they're doing to Farringale while we're dithering out here.'

'I told them we can't wait,' Jay agreed. 'This mess is out of our hands. That mess—' he pointed at the portal—'is entirely our problem.'

Right. I squared my shoulders, too, a smaller, feistier version of Rob. 'I'll go in first,' I said.

Both men looked at me, and I could see questions and objections crystallising in their faces.

I held up a hand. 'Hear me out. I know I said the baroness will help us, but we've got to reach her first. And you're right, if we waltz straight through we'll probably be spotted immediately.' I wondered how Baroness Tremayne had got in and out, presumably without being observed. But she was a griffin. She had other, skyborne pathways. 'I expect Milady told her where we'd be going in. She'll be waiting for us nearby. So I'll just—Merlin in, and let her know we're here.'

'Merlin in,' Jay said.

'Yes.'

'I wasn't aware that "Merlin" was a verb.'

'If that's an oblique way of asking me how I propose to accomplish this feat, I can only tell you: accidentally, via means I can neither anticipate nor plan for.'

I saw the escapade of the Fairy Stone pass behind Jay's eyes, not to mention the episode with the chair. 'This is—haphazard,' he objected.

'I know.'

'Disorganised, uncertain, chaotic, and therefore dangerous.'

'That's me,' I agreed.

He smiled in spite of himself. 'I meant dangerous to *you.*'

'Do you have a better idea?' I hated to challenge him with the deal-breaking *what-else-would-you-suggest* manoeuvre, it's crude. But we were not furnished with a great many options, nor with a great deal of time in which to laboriously reject most of them.

Jay didn't like it either. His smile vanished into grimness: his stare was flinty. 'If you get killed,' he said ominously, 'I'll—'

'Get Zareen to wake me up just so you can kill me again,' I finished for him.

'No. I'll mourn you for the rest of my life.' It was said very seriously, with real feeling.

Ouch. That hit me where it hurts. 'I promise,' I said, really meaning it. 'I'll be careful as pie.'

'As pie? Careful as pie? Pies are *easy* but I never heard they were *careful*—Ves!'

While he was busy muddling his way through my very mixed simile, I was off, striding for that beckoning nimbus of light with all the courage I couldn't quite muster. I'd spoken with outrageous certainty, as though I had any real control over these accidental brilliancies of mine. I hadn't been trying to turn into a Fairy Stone, or a chair either; what made me think I could *accidentally-on-purpose* stealth my way into Farringale via some mysteriously mystical means, and without getting caught?

Only the fact that I'd lucked or catastrophised my way into—and out of—a lot of interesting situations already. And that was before someone had been mad enough to make a Merlin of me.

This jumble of doubts and hopes drained away as I neared the portal, for I was assailed by a—by a deep, shimmering, compelling *awareness* of it, and of the land beyond, that briefly shocked me into immobility. This certainly hadn't happened before. My senses were awash with magick, and with Farringale: the scents and sights of its golden-paved streets and overgrown gardens; water, fresh and chill, or sharply, greenly stagnant; the mulch of old earth, the perfume of spring roses—those damned roses were everywhere—I inhaled, closing my eyes, and I could almost see the winding streets, the grand boulevards, the timber-framed townhouses. That sky. That *sky*, twilight-coloured and roiling with angry, devastating, glorious golden clouds.

Warmth wreathed my limbs, a warmth that came—I thought—from the light itself. The gentle warmth of an afternoon in early summer, like bathing in liquid sunshine.

I felt no movement; there was no sensation of passage. Time passed, and I knew, in some distant way, that I had gone out of England, and into Farringale; that I was a part of it, like a tree rooted in the deep earth; like a stream rushing, bubbling through grassy banks; like a rose, petals unfurled to drink in the sun.

5

Whisht.

The sound broke in upon my reverie. Light splintered.

I woke up, partially.

I wasn't Ves just then. I couldn't have said what I had done with my eyes or my limbs or my fabulous hair, nor what shape I presently wore. I felt at ease with the landscape, as though I had grown there. Perhaps I had.

Cordelia Vesper, came the voice again, and I had regained enough of myself to recognise Baroness Tremayne's tones.

How she perceived me in that state, I couldn't imagine.

Baroness? I attempted to reply.

I sense you but I see nothing of you. How comes this about?

I mulled over how to answer that, when I had so little information myself. What had I done, exactly? What did I look like, just then? *I'll explain later,* I decided, for time pressed, and I had no idea how long I had spent in my sunlit haze. *Can you get Jay and Rob in, without their being seen? They're waiting just outside the portal.*

Cannot you?

Fair question, that. Since I had no real idea what I had done to myself, I had no real idea how to do the same to anyone else—nor even if it were possible. *I was hoping you could take all of us into the echoes,* I went on, ignoring that question too.

A moment.

A flash and a sickening shift; I felt wrenched out of the earth, like an uprooted tree.

Golden light dimmed to a pale, muted silver, and the soft sounds of the city—birdsong, the wind through ancient eaves, and, somewhere, voices—faded. I felt swaddled in mist, my senses muffled.

I had passed into the baroness's strange world.

'*Ves,*' someone was calling, thin, distorted sounds, as though we hung suspended underwater. Jay. He was here somewhere.

I steadied myself with a breath or two, and looked about me. The baroness had moved me in distance as well as time; I stood in a white-walled room, small by troll standards. A single armchair rested, lonely, in a corner, besides which the chamber bore scant decoration: a plain stone mantel crowned a narrow fireplace; shelves built into the walls might once have held books; the bare boards of the floor might once have been covered with a cheerful rug. Perhaps I was in one of those modest merchant's townhouses I'd seen on a prior visit. Shadows flickered oddly in the corners, light crackled and shifted; I blinked, shaking my head. I don't know how Baroness Tremayne has contrived to live in this odd, mutable space for so many years. Perhaps she finds solidity disconcerting, now.

A door stood open opposite me, and in another moment Jay barrelled through it. 'There you are,' he said, with palpable relief.

My heart eased a notch at the sight of him. 'Is Rob with you?'

He jerked his head in terse reply: behind him.

I couldn't see the baroness, but this was her turf: she, of all of us, could be relied upon to handle it.

Her voice emanated out of nowhere even as I framed the thought, and I jumped. *Art prepared?*

Were we prepared. For what? Disasters innumerable and unnameable? Almost certain catastrophe? Slight, but not insignificant risk of actual death?

Eh, probably. I've got used to calling that "Tuesday".

'Art prepared,' I answered firmly. 'Ready for mission briefing.'

This puzzled the baroness; there was a palpable pause. I'd forgotten, for a moment, how she lived—giving new meaning to the term "out of touch". 'Occupation,' she said after a moment, 'seems centred around the library, though there are pockets of activity in other places.'

The library. Of course, the first thing these people had done upon invading Farringale was take control of the library.

Although... I frowned, rapidly revising my ideas. The first thing *I* would do upon invading a sovereign territory—however empty—would be to take over the library. But this wasn't me. 'Who are these people,' I muttered, though I was beginning to develop an idea. If the library was their first, or even sole, objective, then they were a lot like us—only more ruthless.

'Three guesses,' said Jay.

'Too generous,' put in Rob.

I was beginning to agree. If I didn't find Fenella Beaumont somewhere at the back of this mess, I might be eating a couple of hats.

I sighed. 'Let's go to the library, then,' words I usually uttered with more genuine joy, it has to be said.

I braced myself against another sickening lurch through space and time, but nothing happened. 'Tis but a short distance,' the baroness told us. 'This is the librarians' quarters.'

I imagined a complex of dormitories, like a university campus, all housing the multitudinous librarians that must once have staffed the sprawling archives of Farringale: part of a bustling hive of intellectual activity, the likes of which the world may never have seen again. The shattering tragedy of its loss hit me afresh.

'Oh,' said Jay, realisation dawning, as I continued to stand there. 'I'm up.'

'Delighted as I generally am to lead,' I confirmed, 'I'm still me.' Merlin or not, I still couldn't find my way out of a paper bag without assistance.

Jay went to the door and passed out of the room, Rob motioning me to follow. He brought up the rear, guarding us, I supposed, from threats materialising behind us. Strange feeling; Farringale, as yet, seemed almost as empty as it had ever been, the only signs of other life hitherto being a faint babble of voices—and only then when I'd been merged with the land, Merlin-style. It felt almost like playing some kind of game; let's pretend we're on a quest to save a lost kingdom from a terrifying threat. I'll be Merlin, you can be a Waymaster of indescribable power...

I followed Jay into a large vestibule, high of ceiling, with a pair of griffin statues flanking the tall door to the outside. Jay went straight out; I paused only to pat one of the statues on its smooth stone head as I passed. I couldn't have said why. It seemed friendly.

The moment we stepped outside, all my comforting notions of make-believe fell into tatters.

Someone whisked past the librarian's house, close enough to touch Jay: he halted abruptly. My heart stuttered; for an agonising moment I expected to be seen, to be caught; then the odd dimness of the noontide light, the shimmering, flickering haze over everything we saw, reminded me that we were undetectable. Hopefully.

We waited in brief, frozen silence, immobile—my mind spiralled back into childhood games and Granny's Footsteps—a most inapposite desire to giggle rose in me, and I choked it down. The pressure was making me hysterical.

The person, whoever it was, passed by at a near-run, and it struck me that the hive of activity I'd been imagining moments before had returned to Farringale after all. If only they weren't uninvited, irresponsible, and destructive—

'This way,' Jay whispered, stepping confidently out. I trailed after, heart pounding—it takes serious nerve to wander down a street, out in the open, and just trust that nobody will be able to see you.

Nobody did, but we saw plenty. Jay led us on a short, winding route around a cluster of stone-built houses—the rest of the librarians' quarters, I supposed—and several people passed us, moving at considerable speed.

Now that we were closer, I was able to see that they were carrying armfuls of stuff. Books.

'They're stripping the library,' I hissed, a surge of such rage swelling my heart that I couldn't breathe.

'I feel bound to point out that we did the same thing,' Jay said. 'Not that I mean to defend *them*, of course.'

'We did not. We took several books, and only to save them. They're taking—everything—' I shut up, and breathed.

'Maybe they're saving them,' Rob put in, but in a dry tone.

I scoffed audibly at that. 'Of course they are. Zero personal interest involved.'

They were all human, these bustling thieves, which did not surprise me. Though the notable lack of any trolls did interest me a little: was that mere happenstance, or had these invaders known about the state of Farringale, known that any trolls they brought here would be in severe danger?

The existence of the ortherex; the fate of Farringale, and other Troll Enclaves; these things were not secrets, exactly. It had taken a huge, concerted effort to save some of the beleaguered Enclaves, involving the Society, the Troll Court, and other organisations; word of it must surely have spread.

Still. This was looking more and more like a carefully planned operation by somebody with considerable information. Someone who'd been paying close attention to what *we* had been doing this past year.

We turned a corner, and the library rose before us: a statuesque construct, a cathedral to knowledge, its gleaming white walls glittering with glass. Another person came barrelling out of the entrance as we watched and hurtled down the steps, a woman with soft brown hair, an armful of books, and a harried expression. They weren't wasting any time: clearly they expected this incursion wouldn't remain a secret for long.

Was this their only goal? Robbing the library?

Would that alone have rattled the unflappable baroness so?

Jay stealthed up the wide stone steps to the entrance, neatly evading further bandits dashing out with more books. I wondered where they were taking them, pictured trucks driven up to the gates of Farringale somewhere and filled up with stolen material. What a coup—if they could pull it off.

I smothered a rebellious corner of my soul that traitorously wished *we* had thought to come here with trucks and empty the library—there were reasons why we hadn't, we had ethics and standards and we didn't *do* this sort of thing, let it go, Ves—and followed Jay up the stairs.

Inside, chaos reigned.

On our last visit here, the library had been shrouded in dust and silence, like Sleeping Beauty's enchanted tower. Spellbound, as though the city had fallen asleep, and might wake at any moment.

Now it bustled with the worst kind of activity. Easily twenty people were looting the shelves, hastily, haphazardly, scooping armloads of delicate tomes onto the floor and shoving them into boxes. Others merely grabbed eight or ten off the nearest shelf and ran for the door. I winced at the *thud, thudding* as more and more books fell off their shelves and landed in crashing heaps, sending waves of dust into the air.

Rage set my heart afire; I could have screamed my fury.

As much as I could understand the desire to loot every single page of precious knowledge out of the lost library of Farringale, I could never condone *this*—this—this travesty, this *piracy*. Nobody cared if the books were damaged during this shambles of a process; nor did they care that the right of ownership over them was emphatically not theirs.

They weren't emptying the great library of Farringale; they were destroying it.

My feelings were echoed in Jay and Rob, for the three of us stood frozen in shared horror for some minutes. It defied belief, that anybody with a value for knowledge could treat the place with such a total lack of respect—how *could* they—

'Right,' I said, crisply, and the syllable contained worlds of steely resolution.

'Right,' Jay agreed, grim as death.

Rob merely nodded. We were agreed. Whatever it took, we were stopping these people.

But we were here on reconnaissance only. We didn't have the numbers to mount a counter offensive, and it would take days to muster that kind of a force and get it all the way down here (we had only the one Waymaster, and there was no conceivable way Jay could be expected to cart a hundred Society members across such a distance).

By the haste with which these thieves were working, they knew this. They weren't planning to be here in a few days' time; they were getting the goods and getting out. By the time reinforcements arrived, it would be too late—at least for the library.

If there was ever a good time to go catastrophically, devastatingly Merlin on somebody, this was it.

6

'WHAT'S THE PLAN,' JAY whispered to me as we stood there, frozen with horror amidst the destruction of the great library of Farringale.

'I don't know,' I admitted, already reaching with those other senses, hooking my mind and my heart into the landscape around me. 'I think I'm about to wing it.'

If he replied, I didn't hear it. My consciousness winged away from him, from Rob; away from the hideous spectacle of looters emptying those long-neglected shelves; brushed past Mauf, still asleep in my satchel—a mercy upon him; I left him undisturbed—past Baroness Tremayne, a distressed shadow haunting the scene, just out of sight or hearing; sank at last into the bones of the earth below.

Trees. I joined a tangle of their deep roots, a web running beneath the paved streets and stone houses, oak and ash and elm; we'd seen some few of them flanking the library, their heavy boughs still shading the deserted boulevards, long ages after those who had planted them had gone.

Something else lingered there: a memory, a ghost; trees-that-were, once; had ceased to grow, ceased to soak up the sunlight and rainfall of Farringale. The last of their sweet, spring leaves lay far behind them: hundreds of years had passed since they had last borne fruit, borne seed, let their green leaves turn the colour of amber and drift down into the slow death of autumn.

They had not forgotten. The memories lay locked inside every knot, every whorl, and I realised at last what it was I had encountered.

Shelves. The bookshelves of the library of Farringale had been built here, out of the siblings of those same trees that rose so proudly outside: and they were trees still, somewhere inside.

An idea unfurled in my own mind, like a leaf in spring: fresh and lovely and perfect. It was the work of a moment to touch those slumbering sparks with a thread of magick, to whisper to them of light, and fresh-fallen water. They responded, stretching themselves as they woke, reaching with fresh life and growth for the heavens.

And the leaves of Farringale—the thousands, hundreds of thousands, of bound and inked and printed pages, each one pressed from the mulch that had once, also, been a tree—these they carried with them, unfurling them like banners, opened to the sun.

I came back to myself slowly, through a greater exertion of effort than it had cost me to lose myself, for that little space of time. How simple, how easy, the life of a tree: the slow turning of the seasons around me, the crisp freshness of rainwater, the dulcet warmth of sunlight upon my up-turned leaves...

In what stark, sharp contrast, the life of a Ves: hurry and haste, pain and turmoil, pressure and distress—I *liked* being a tree, could easily come to prefer it over any other shape—I fought to grasp the beauties of my little human life, the details: strong cups of tea in the morning, with lashings of milk; carrot cake, and Bakewell tarts; dance par-ties at midnight, when I couldn't sleep—*hugs*, preferably from Jay; the velvety softness of Addie's nose; the snap in Milady's voice when I'd displeased her—

I flailed, halfway Ves and halfway tree, and then some-one was shaking me, shouting my name in my ears and—

I had eyes again; I felt them; I opened them.

Jay, a vision of concerned fury. I was still a creature of heightened and layered senses, every pore tuned to the myriad cues of my environment. I felt every wave of Jay's distress, felt it begin to ebb, when he saw me looking back at him.

'We are really going to have to talk about this,' he growled at me, his fingers digging into my shoulders where—I concluded—he had been shaking me.

'Agreed,' I breathed, gulping air. The ease with which I meld with landscapes, turn myself into boulders and bridges and chairs—it's exhilarating, in the same way as a rollercoaster, the kind where you're only *mostly* certain that you aren't going to go hurtling off the rails at the next corner, and sail off into oblivion, screaming.

If I could only turn myself *back* with the same ease I wouldn't mind it half so much.

'Was I a tree?' I whispered, half afraid of the answer.

'Something like that—' began Jay.

'Ves,' Rob broke in, and I tore my gaze away from my fascinated scrutiny of Jay's expressions. 'Was that you? I really hope that was you.'

He gestured, widely, and I beheld, with some awe, the fruits of my impromptu labours.

The library-as-was would, in all likelihood, never be the same again. The bookcases were gone, the very walls had shifted, and the roof gaped open to let the sky in; I wondered distantly what had become of the rafters, not to mention the roof tiles.

A forest had sprung up out of the earth. Chiefly oaks, these handsome trees: not so very old yet, their trunks still slight and lithe, but they were growing, thickening: changing, changing *back*, into the grand old trees they had been long ago, before men of Farringale had come with axes, and chopped them down.

A thick canopy shaded us from sun and wind: a rustling, green arbour, smelling of spring, and among those unfurling leaves there were: books.

I breathed out, a note of relief, for I had not, in my haste and carelessness, disassembled every book in the library, turning every separate page into roots and leaves. The books looked intact, as far as I could tell from some distance below: hanging from the branches like tempting fruits, far out of reach.

I watched as a quick-thinking looter jumped, reaching for a low-hanging tome; his hands never closed upon it, for the tree snatched it back, quick as lightning. The earth shook in palpable warning.

'Yes, but before you ask,' I informed Rob, and Jay, 'No, I don't have the slightest idea how I am going to get them down from there.'

'Noted,' said Jay.

'But they seem to be safe, for the moment.' So I fervently hoped; it was always possible that I had done as much damage to the books with my magick as the thieves had with their careless, grabbing hands, but I couldn't think of that now. It was too late. I would have to hope that the love and fear I had laced into my magick had preserved them; the trees' obvious protectiveness of their bookish burdens boded well.

Of course, I had been anything but subtle. Only some of the book thieves' attention remained upon their prize, now hanging out of reach; others were raising the alarm, shouting questions at each other, beginning a search for the culprit. For me.

They wouldn't find us: not yet, not while we remained tucked behind the echoes of space and time, swaddled in shadows and silence. But we couldn't stay that way, and we had other objectives before we could hasten back to the Society.

I paused long enough to watch as several more energetic souls attempted various methods of retrieving the hanging books: jumping; boosting each other on cupped hands, or shoulders; climbing into the boughs of the trees themselves. All failed: the trees retaliated, swatting and swiping away the climbers, or shaking the looters out of their branches.

'Right,' said Jay, shaking himself out of his absorbed appreciation of the scene. 'We need to find out what's become of the regulators.'

The regulators, freshly ripped from Silvessen and—what? What were these people intending to do with them in Farringale? Whatever it was, I didn't think they had yet deployed them. Surely there would be some sign already, some shift in the conditions of Farringale. Or would there? Could two regulators have much of an effect on an entire, magick-drowned city?

Someone passed by me, almost close enough to touch, and my train of thought shattered—I *knew* him, I was sure of it—shadowed as he was in my sight, his movements juddery and jerky, the strange effect of my disconnected state—even so—I followed him at a trot, noting his height, the breadth of his shoulders, the public schoolboy cut of his hair—

'That's George Mercer,' I hissed, and stamped my foot in sheer rage. 'Ancestria bloody Magicka.'

'You're certain?' Jay called, following me.

'Yes. I suppose he might have defected to some other soulless organisation devoted to the plunder of magickal heritage, but I doubt it.'

Jay seemed unsurprised, and so was I. Fenella sodding Beaumont: she just couldn't go more than a month or two without kicking up fresh trouble.

Rob was hulking. It's a squared-shoulders, chin-raised, threatening sort of posture he does when he's contemplating destroying someone (to do him justice, he hardly ever actually does).

'Now's not the time,' I told him. He'd have to step out from behind the echoes to actually lay hands—or Wands—on Mercer directly, and we were vastly outnumbered in here.

Rob gave me a terse nod, and his shoulders relaxed. 'We'd better get a move on,' he told me. 'I may be wrong, but I think we have a surge coming on.'

I glanced at what was left of the library's mullioned windows, forest-bound as they now were. I might have imagined it, but was that a slow flush of pale colour creeping across the glass? A soft, palpable hum of magick building in the air?

'That seems—' I began, but was unable to finish the sentence for the sheer sinking of my heart. It seemed like improbably prompt timing, but what if it wasn't random? I *had* just unleashed a small tidal wave of magick in the great library. I'd turned the previously inert bookshelves into Merlin-trees, and now that I had occasion to think about it they *were* rather fizzy with magick—

'Oh, dear,' I sighed, exchanging one fraught glance with Jay. The same realisation was written all over his face.

'It'll be all right,' he said reassuringly. 'We've weathered these surges before.'

We had, but that was before I'd emerged from the fifth Britain in a state of dangerous magickal excess. Before I'd set eyes—or hands—on the strange old lyre from my mother's Yllanfalen kingdom. Before I'd become a Merlin. No one could say what the effect would now be upon my shrinking self.

I had two choices. Wait and see—or run away.

I took a big breath, squared my shoulders, and hulked. 'It'll be okay,' I echoed Jay, trying to sound like I meant it.

I could feel it now, pulsing through the floor under my shoes and thrumming in the air.

From the depths of my satchel, an irate voice began shouting. '*Miss Vesper. Permit me to ask—with the utmost esteem and respect for your ordinarily unimpeachable judgement—what in the name of every conceivable god have you done to my LIBRARY.*'

Mauf had woken up. And I saw his point fairly quickly, for quite apart from the unusual elevation of the formerly neat rows of books there was something else going on. They were—swaying. Their pages were fluttering, as though riffled by invisible fingers. As I watched, a cloud of butterflies erupted from the pages of one handsome old tome, and exploded in tiny flashes of light.

A discordant chorus of babbling voices rose in volume, rising with the magickal tide: the books of Farringale were gibbering, cackling, screaming in rage—

--And then, horror of horrors, the bright young oaks I'd conjured out of the bookshelves ripped their roots out of the earth and began to walk.

7

THE LAST TIME I'D experienced one of Farringale's mag-ickal surges, the effects had been entertaining as much as they'd been alarming. Indira had flown, quite literally, like a bird. Rob had conjured creatures of scintillating light out of the tip of his Lapis Wand, and sent them soaring about the library. I'd turned myself into a pancake. The fact that we'd all been so totally out of control of ourselves hadn't been *great*, with hindsight, but none of us had been inclined to do anything dangerous.

This, though. *This* was something else.

My lovely, flourishing trees, books hanging from their branches like streamers, roots tearing out of the earth with appalling rumbling, crashing, *cracking* sounds—those trees were *angry*.

'Oh,' I said numbly, spellbound with horror. I watched as several trees mustered themselves into formation and—eight thousand books screaming in cacophonous concert—ran at the hapless looters.

Not that so many of the latter had stuck around for it. About half had left the library after my impromptu intervention, probably to seek advice, and most of the rest had sensibly legged it the moment the first tree had torn itself loose.

George Mercer was among the foolhardy souls who re-mained. For a split second, I felt glad—let him pay for his many offences, a good skewering wouldn't be unde-served—but I thought better of it almost immediately.

I was responsible for this. If I hadn't interfered, there might have been no surge happening at all; and if there had, there'd have been no ornery oaks on the warpath, feeling a wee bit bitter about being hacked down and turned into shelves. I didn't want to be the reason somebody died today.

An enraged oak thundered past far too close—Jay hauled me out of the way, thankfully before we could establish whether or not their fury extended all the way through the echoes of memory and time. I felt a strong *whoosh* of air as it passed; shock had me clinging, just for a moment, to Jay.

'Thanks,' I gasped, and took off running.

What I was planning to do, I couldn't have said. I couldn't hear Mauf anymore, not over the tumult of vituperative voices, but his indignant presence at my side was an extra spur as I shot into the heart of the library, dodging warring trees and fleeing agents of Ancestria Magicka. At least I had thoroughly disrupted their plundering party: nobody would be trying to touch *those* books anymore.

I ran through chambers that had once held thousands of books, several somnolent birch or elm or ash trees still slumbering in the corners. I was making for the room we'd come to think of as the museum: an unfathomably tall-ceilinged space filled with artefacts behind glass, the lost relics of a vanished Troll Court. There would be no trees in there, most likely, for there hadn't been any bookcases: only starstone and glass.

I found it intact, and—relatively—peaceful. The cacophony of disaster went on beyond the rounded archways, all too audible; I winced at a particularly devastating crash. Small hope that the books weren't coming to collective, and terrible, grief: my fault, too.

'Mauf,' I gasped, dropping to the floor, and hauling him out of my satchel.

'I cannot sufficiently express the extent of my disappointment,' shouted the book, and snapped—actually snapped—at my fingers.

'I know, I *know*. I'm sorry. I intended none of this to happen, and you've got to help me stop it.'

'It cannot be stopped!' shrieked Mauf, rather hysterically. 'These blundersome, quarrelsome creatures are beyond anyone's control.' He began, shockingly, to sob. 'My books. My poor, poor books...'

'Never mind the books right now,' I snapped back. 'We'll mend them. Later. We need to focus on the *trees*.' I thumped the heavy weight of him smartly against the floor: the equivalent of a ringing slap. 'Focus, Mauf. I need your help here.'

The wrenching sobs stopped, to my relief. A long moment's silence followed, before he said, much more coolly, 'Logic suggests that, when the surging of magick in these environs should ebb, then the trees will settle.'

'It does suggest that,' I agreed, 'but that may be some time in happening.'

'Then the best thing to do would be to turn them back into bookcases—' His words cut off as I abruptly slammed his covers closed again, struck with a piece of genius I hadn't, in the end, needed Mauf for.

'I could,' I answered him rapidly, 'I think. Maybe. But that would just put us right back where we were, wouldn't it? This is Ancestria Magicka we're dealing with. They aren't going to slink away like whipped dogs just because a couple of trees tried to butcher them like pigs. The moment the trees are gone, the shelves are back, and the books are accessible, they'll be out the door with the lot.'

Mauf uttered something, rather muffled. '—fear you are contemplating further madness—entreat you to see reason—'

'You're quite right,' I told him, stuffing him back into my satchel. 'I am contemplating madness.' Possibly the magick was getting to my brain by then, for I was far too pleased with myself, grinning like an idiot, and nowhere near as sensible of the risks as I should have been.

I laid my palms against the buzzing starstone floor, felt the ripples and waves of burgeoning magick shocking the atmosphere. It was easy, in that environment: barely cost me a thought.

Poor Jay came haring into the museum just an instant too late. I was already growing taller—much, *much* taller—my trunk thickening, arms and tendrils of hair lengthening into lithe, supple boughs. My eaves bristled with a glittering crop of silver leaves, and as I shook myself a spray of purple fruits flew out and splattered across the walls.

'VES!' Jay bawled at me from a long way below. 'You can't do this—come back from there, this is insane, what are you *thinking*—'

I heard no more, for I picked up my winding roots and stomped off, causing only a little damage to an unoffending wall in the process.

I'd already noticed that these trees seemed to possess the capacity to order themselves. They'd formed up like a battalion, attacked in concert—and that meant they could be lead.

By, for example, me.

'FORM. UP,' I roared, though it wasn't words that reached them. I rumbled and crashed in a cacophony of bough and branch, a roar of spraying earth and shaken, shattering leaves: and they heard.

I'd popped out from between the echoes, I distantly realised—burst out of it, a shattering tide of magick too vast to be contained—swollen with Farringale's own disordered currents, burgeoning into an unstoppable wave.

Nobody stopped me. Nobody could have, in that moment. I stomped out of the wreck of the library and away down the bright white boulevard, a pied piper of the forest, with a legion of irate trees stamping along in my wake.

What tales they might tell of this in days to come: the thought came to me dimly, prompted by the awed stares—nay, *flabbergasted*—I was receiving from Ancestria Magicka's rotten agents as we passed (just before they scurried out of my path, like rats deserting the proverbial sinking ship).

The legend of Farringale, already a place of myth, story and song, had just grown a little larger and more improbable. I smiled to think of it, somewhere beneath leaf and bark, for as strange a story as they'd tell of this day, the truth was stranger still.

We were out of Farringale and halfway to Winchester before I faltered, paused, and, ultimately, stopped. Fields surrounded us, rippling with burgeoning wheat, or barley, perhaps: a verdant blanket of growth, dotted with copses of my fellow oaks and birches and yews. I turned about, spirits sinking with the velocity of a brick turfed off a tall building.

'Um,' I uttered in a rustle of silverish leaves. 'Does anybody know the way to Mandridore?'

THE DAY MAY YET come when I'll be so used to Ves's antics as to feel no surprise, however mad her methodology.

That day is a ways off, I reckon.

Yelling sense at Ves as she *turns herself into a gods-forsaken tree* and strides away: why did I imagine that would work? Off she went regardless, tossing her leafy canopy in a maddeningly Ves-like gesture despite the arboreal format and for a painfully long minute, Rob and I were left in frozen silence.

Rob permitted himself an audible sigh.

'What's interesting is,' I said at length, 'she seems to have taken most of the magick with her.' The magickal surge that had been steadily building was ebbing away again, and perhaps that wasn't so surprising. I couldn't even dimly imagine the power it must have taken Ves to perform those several improbable feats in such quick succession.

'She's going to need help,' said Rob.

I blinked, and straightened. Good point. Where in the name of her giddy gods did she imagine she was going with the library of Farringale? 'Perhaps she can, I don't know—' I spread my hands in a hopeful gesture—'Merlin her way to somewhere?'

Rob just looked at me.

'Right. No, you're right.' Ves might be magickal beyond sense, marvellous beyond reason, and impossibly, dazzlingly competent, but she was still Ves. She'd be lost inside of half an hour.

I succumbed to a momentary burst of panic. I wanted to dash after her instantly—she needed me—but I couldn't just abandon Farringale. Ves herself would kill me if we bombed out of there without completing the mission.

We'd have to get a move on.

'Regulators first,' I said. 'Then Ves.'

'Thought,' said Rob. 'Griffins.'

I nodded. The notable lack of them as we'd come in had struck me forcibly, only to be swept out of my mind by the chaos that had immediately ensued. There were several that lived atop Mount Farringale, not far beyond the borders of the city. They'd violently opposed our entry, the first time we'd stepped through the portal. Why hadn't they dealt with Ancestria Magicka?

'Oh no,' said I, struck by a horrible thought. 'You don't suppose they used the regulators—?'

I couldn't finish the thought in any detail: just what might they have used the regulators to do as regarded the griffins? *Something*, anyway: the likelihood that those regulators were here *and* the griffins unaccountably missing, purely by coincidence, was slim. They had to be related.

Rob nodded grimly. 'Baroness? Do you know what's become of the griffins?'

A long pause followed, and I began to fear we'd lost her somewhere. But then she spoke: '*One is no more; two are captured. The rest bide yet in Farringale, but they are ensorcelled.*'

I wished, fleetingly, that we had brought Indira after all: my sister would know at once how they had used Orlando's regulators to ensorcel—or capture, or kill—a griffin. 'Where are they?' I asked.

'*Come,*' she said briefly, and the shadowed shape of her flickered into view, limned in pallid light. She led us away from the library, through streets largely deserted, now; wherever Ancestria Magicka had gone, their attempts to divest the city of its knowledge had been permanently foiled, to Ves's credit.

We didn't need to go far. A few minutes' slinking around shadowed corners brought us to a kind of stables, or mews: rows of tall, handsome stone buildings arrayed around a square courtyard, grand in both size and style. Once upon a time, horses and perhaps even unicorns had resided here, I supposed, along with those who cared for them.

The stalls stood empty, as far as I could see, but the courtyard bustled with activity.

Three griffins crouched there, bound in a strange kind of lassitude: not asleep, quite, but fuddled, dreaming. So secure was their confinement that they were not even bound, save by a shackle chained around one furred leg, and attached to the stone walls.

Several people lingered near them, only a little wary of demeanour: with a wave of fury I recognised Fenella Beaumont. She was playing overseer, three of her henchmen engaged in the operation of one of Orlando's regulators: I could feel the odd pulse of its magick thrumming through the floor.

It took me a moment longer to realise what else was so wrong with this scene. The griffins, hunched in their demi-slumber, lay inert: not so much as a flicker of lightning wreathed those handsome, feathered forms. That was what the regulators had done; of course it was. The griffins were the magickal heart of Farringale, the source—we surmised—of its deep, wild magick, and the regulators had—well—*regulated* them.

Helped along, doubtless, by Ancestria Magicka, with the specific aim of subduing them.

I took a long, slow breath, too consumed with fury to speak—at least for a moment.

'Well,' I said at last. 'It's maybe a good thing Ves isn't here to see this.'

8

IT TOOK ME ALTOGETHER too long to remember a couple of things—which, I might as well add, would have been immediately apparent to Jay (not to mention Indira).

One: I was travelling with a small forest, yes, but said forest had one of the greatest libraries in the world dangling from its swaying branches.

Two: I might not have been similarly festooned with knowledge, but I did still have Mauf somewhere about my person.

'Does anyone know the way to Mandridore?' I'd said, not really expecting a response.

Response, however, there had been: an immediate susurration of rustling leaves—tree chatter—had gone up, with a babble of ancient, learnèd voices mixed up somewhere therein.

—thou'rt a fool; it is not westerly, thou hast the pages upside down—

—manner of nonsense is this. Ha! Mandridore! There is no such place, nor has ever been—

—past Mount Battle and over the River Winding—

And over the top of this babble, Mauf's refined accents raised to a near roar: 'My good tomes and volumes—my very dear lexicons and folios—WE are the greatest library this world has ever known. Such conduct is highly unbecoming of our situation in life.'

The chatter did not appreciably lessen, but Mauf went on, inexorably shouting over them: 'IF you would be so good as to hold your tongues, all of you, I believe we may swiftly find our way to a resolution of Merlin's little difficulty.'

I didn't immediately recognise myself by the name Merlin—I required a moment's reflection, for that—but it was clever of Mauf to use it. These ancient volumes could never have received any information about the Society, nor would they care; but Merlin, that was another matter. The books' quarrelling stopped, became instead an excited babble in which that hallowed name, *Merlin,* was many times repeated.

'Precisely,' said Mauf, at a more decorous volume. 'Merlin. Shall you now comport yourselves with some dignity?'

The books, duly shamed, fell largely silent, barring an occasional rustle of pages—and one, slightly disturbing giggle.

'Thank you. Now then. Mandridore, as most of you will not know, is as Farringale once was: the great, and very grand home of Their Majesties, Queen Ysurra and King Naldran, noble heirs as they are to Their Majesties Hrruna and Torvaston; seat of the Troll Court, and therefore, home to the *current* Great Library of Magick. And if you would like to be restored to your rightful places upon such august shelves, you will assist me in directing Merlin to the gates of Mandridore forthwith, and without further ado.' Mauf paused, and added, 'The next volume to *giggle* shall instead be cast into the nearest brackish stream.'

The giggling, mercifully, cut off with a choking sound.

'Thank you. Now. Which among you contain maps of England?'

Several books piped up.

'And which among you contain some manner of reference to the Old Roads of the Court?'

'The what—' I put in, but stopped as the answer occurred to me. The Troll Roads. He was talking about the magickal Ways I'd once or twice travelled over of late, usu- ally with Baron Alban. 'Oooh, that's clever,' I said instead.

Mauf radiated a quiet, smug pleasure. 'Yes, it is. Do not worry, Miss Vesper. We shall have you in Mandridore in a trice.'

THEY DID, AS WELL. I was obliged to promise, later, that I would not say exactly how; such knowledge is for the rar- efied few, and those tomes whose pages offer some useful clue will doubtless disappear very quickly into Mandri- dore's protected archives.

I can only say that our little ambulatory forest was very soon in motion again, and it was not long before we were out of England Proper and sauntering joyously down the wide, rose-strewn boulevards that the trolls built long, long ago.

Had I been obliged to walk those Ways as myself, I would have tired in due time, for despite the Way-wending magicks infused into the white stones of those roads, the journey was a considerable one. I did not tire, though, as a tree; a tree has no muscles, that can grow weary with use. I was powered by magick, and not only my own: the fizzing, ferocious magick of over-burdened Farringale was in me still, and wafted me with the greatest ease all the way to Mandridore.

We caused rather a stir, let me tell you. It's not every day an entire copse of English trees in full and varied leaf trundles en masse through the gilded gates of the Court Enclave. We accumulated curious followers as we went, and by the time we stopped outside the palace we had an entourage at least as large in number as we were.

Things became somewhat confused after that. I recall being ushered, by what means I know not, into the vast formal gardens that lie behind the palace, into which my arboreal fellows cheerfully dispersed. I must have dropped into a doze, I suppose, for such an excess of magick cannot help but weary a woman eventually.

I drifted out of slumber again to find myself parked in a quiet corner of the queen's garden, flanked by fragrant orange trees, and with an ornate stone bench positioned under my eaves. Two people were seated upon it: the soft murmur of their conversation had woken me.

'—most spectacular thing I've ever seen,' Jay was saying. 'I haven't the slightest idea how she thought of it.'

'She's Ves,' answered Alban. 'Her mind works in mysterious ways.'

'Turned the whole damned library into a forest and walked off with it.' Jay was shaking his head. 'Some damage to the building in the process, of course, but nothing the Court can't fix.'

'They won't object to that. Not when Ves has brought them the entire lost library of Farringale.'

Not the entire library, I tried to say, without success: my leaves rustled frenetically, but no words emerged.

Both faces looked up into my branches. 'Have another go,' said Jay, laying a hand against my trunk.

I did, with much the same result.

'I hope you aren't planning to remain a tree forever,' Alban said. 'Not that you aren't a splendid, majestic tree, of course.'

'The very best of trees,' Jay agreed. 'But there's a cup of tea with your name on it, Ves, and it's getting cold.'

'And a plate of pancakes,' Alban added. 'The enormous ones, with the fruit and the ice cream.'

I rustled a bit more, dropping a purple fruit into Jay's lap, which burst juicily.

Jay looked at it in silence, then said to Alban: 'It's not the entire library. That's probably what she's worried about. Ancestria Magicka took some books before we could stop them.'

'Excellent,' said Alban, in an uncharacteristically grim tone. 'Those books are lawfully the property of the Troll Court. We'll prosecute them for theft.'

'Later. The griffins need help first.'

Griffins? What was amiss with the griffins? My brain exploded with questions; several more fruits sprayed juice over the pristine gravel walk.

'Maybe have those pancakes brought out here,' Jay suggested. 'Where she can see them.'

With careful intent and precise aim, I dropped a fruit on Jay's head.

'You're welcome to do something terrible to me,' Jay correctly interpreted, 'but you'll have to turn human again first.'

I sagged, my branches drooping. *I'd love to turn human again*, I told him (rustle, rustle).

Jay patted my trunk soothingly. 'I know. But if you conquered the chair problem, you can do this, too.'

'Chair problem?' Alban queried.

Jay shook his head. 'Best not to ask.'

THEY BROUGHT OUT THE pancakes. And when those turned cold and congealed, another plate of pancakes—not to mention huge, troll-sized pots of tea. Jay and Alban sat with me for an hour straight, and then another, swapping stories of our escapades, reminding me of my human self.

I chafed under the delay, and so did they, I'm sure, though they hid it well. Something was gravely amiss with the griffins of Farringale; Ancestria Magicka had got away with a lot of the library's books; who-knew-what other mischief was brewing; and I was stuck in the shape of a tree.

Trying to perform difficult, unfamiliar magicks under a sense of intense pressure isn't my preferred way of doing things.

At length—at very great length—my bark softened and became cloth; my leaves and withies dissolved into jade-green coloured hair; and I had eyes again, lips to talk with, arms to wrap around Jay and Alban in the hugest, bone-crushing bear hugs I (in my diminutive frame) could manage.

And questions. I had a lot of *questions.* 'What do you mean about the griffins—thank you, by the way, for all this—*this*—but what's afoot in Farringale—oh, did you find out what became of the regulators?—can we get the lost books back—' I uttered all this in bursts, in between enormous gulps of tea (sweet, and milky), and forkfuls of pancake.

Jay apprised me, fairly succinctly, of the Griffin Problem, which made my blood boil with impotent rage. 'Rob's back at Home, updating Milady,' he concluded. 'I came here to find you, I hoped, and also to report to the Court. We'll need help, at this point. We couldn't take on all of Ancestria Magicka with just the two of us.'

Perhaps he'd read a certain mulish accusation in my face, for that last bit came out slightly defensive. 'I know,' I assured him. 'I wish you could've, but—'

'So do we,' Jay said bleakly, and I saw what it must have cost him to walk away and leave those noble griffins in captivity.

'Their Majesties are holding an emergency council soon,' Alban told me, and checked his watch. 'In about half an hour, in fact.' I burst into speech, and he held up a hand to forestall me. 'Your presence is required, don't worry. We'll need you and Jay to explain the situation at Farringale, and you're to represent the Society while we debate how best to launch a sensible opposition.'

Sensible meaning: they couldn't send many of their own people with us. No troll could safely enter Farringale, not yet. Maybe not ever.

But they were a large, cosmopolitan Enclave: they had people who weren't trolls, and besides that they had some of the brightest minds in the country. We wouldn't have to handle a problem of this magnitude alone.

'That being so,' I said, 'I'd better fortify myself with plentiful comestibles. I'm *hungry*.' In fact I was ravenous: a tree may thrive on sun and water alone, but I couldn't.

Jay handed me another mug of tea, and downed the dregs of his own. 'We're as ready as milk and sugar can make us,' he proclaimed.

Which, I hoped, would be enough.

9

THE FIRST TIME I met the king and queen of the trolls, they were rather informally dressed. They were wearing leisure kit, to be precise—pyjamas, almost (excepting the coronet sported by her gracious majesty Ysurra).

When there's an emergency council of war, though, they bring out the sartorial big guns.

Alban escorted Jay and I into a sort of grand presence chamber, dating, probably, from the 1600s. Its vaulted ceiling swooped away to impossible heights – or so it seemed, from my modest vantage point. Quite a few people occupied an array of silk-upholstered chairs, but the room dwarfed us, the chatter of voices echoing in the emptiness of the space.

Enthroned in the centre—more or less literally—were their joint majesties, King Naldran and Queen Ysurra, draped in sumptuous state regalia. Both were coroneted; both wore robes of crisp silk brocade, and sat with a kind of statuesque posture which couldn't help but seem imposing. I wondered as to the identity of some of the other attendees, several of whom bore the grandeur of visiting dignitaries. Most of them were trolls, but not all: I saw a few other humans, like myself; one or two Yllanfalen; and several fae. I looked for Emellana Rogan, hoping to see her familiar face, but she wasn't there.

Alban seated Jay and I at the front, where we sat feeling like prized exhibits in some grand museum (or I did, anyway; Jay appeared as composed as ever). Alban settled nearby, in between us and their majesties. I felt a little reassured by his familiar bulk so close, like a bulwark against the storm.

Our arrival appeared to signal the beginning of the meeting, for the great double doors were closed behind us (with an echoing *boom*), and King Naldran began to speak.

'We thank you for your prompt attendance of this impromptu council. The matter at hand, as you may imagine, is of some urgency, and does not admit of any delay. I believe everyone here is acquainted with the situation of ancient Farringale; in particular its impassibility, at least by those of the troll people. It has therefore been impossible for us to reclaim the vast wealth of our cultural heritage which remains within its walls, reports of which we have lately received in some detail from the Society.' His august gaze rested, briefly, upon me, and I couldn't help wincing a bit. Here we came to the crux of the matter. He was, thus far, characterising our involvement in positive terms; however I was as aware as he must be that a more negative construction could be placed upon it. If Jay and Alban and I hadn't breached the walls of Farringale a year ago, and carried out tales of its marvels (not to mention examples of it, like Mauf and his predecessor), well then Ancestria Magicka would never have been alerted to its treasures either. And the current incursion probably would never have happened.

The king said none of this, thankfully. 'Unfortunately,' he went on, 'there are those who covet the unique treasures of Farringale, and who are, even now, carrying away some portion of its irreplaceable artefacts. If we do not act, and quickly, we are like to see the total devastation of the priceless heritage of our ancient court. The extent of the cultural loss to the troll people can scarcely be described.'

'We call for aid,' said Queen Ysurra. 'The might of the Troll Court stands at naught in this instance, for our people can only enter Farringale at the greatest cost. Queen Mab assures us the full support of the Society and all its expertise, but against the might and the ruthlessness of Ancestria Magicka it must struggle to prevail alone.'

Queen Mab! I felt a jolt, a shock, to hear that name so openly pronounced. Milady's identity, if it had ever been a secret to these people, was secret no longer.

'Who will answer this call?' continued Ysurra. 'We and all our Court shall stand forever in your debt.'

My hand shot up before I'd had chance to think things through. 'I can promise the assistance of the kingdom of Ygranyllon,' I said, with a confidence it in no way merited, for did not my mother delight in being difficult?

The queen inclined her head at me. 'If they are so inclined, then we are grateful.'

Which was a polite way of saying: if my mother actually backed me up on my promise, great.

She would. I'd get her to help us, by hook or by crook.

I remained silent after that, as others offered aid. The emerging picture proved serious: if I'd been minded to name Ancestria Magicka's move into Farringale as an invasion, well, this was an army mustering in response. If Fenella Beaumont had imagined she could rob the city with impunity, she was sorely mistaken.

She might have imagined just that, I supposed, for had not Farringale been left, all these long centuries, in its abandoned state? A whole year gone by since Jay and I had first set foot in the decaying city, and all its treasures remained therein: untouched. Unwanted?

No, she could never imagine them unwanted. She must know that the Court would exercise its right to the contents of Farringale, as soon as a solution was found to the infestation which rendered it impenetrable to the trolls. That's why she had acted now: before there would be any chance of the entire Troll Court descending in all its fury to oppose her plundering of the city.

What a pity they could not. For all the ready assistance of the Court's allies, there'd be nothing quite like a legion of infuriated trolls to send a wily thief packing. And it was their ancestral home: who had the right, if not they?

'Jay...' I whispered, as voices rose and fell around us, determining the fate of Farringale in a few hastily agreed deals.

'Yes.'

'What if we could...'

He waited, and then prompted: 'Yes?'

'I mean, wouldn't it be *marvellous* if we could...'

He turned his head to look at me when I trailed off again. I knew that my idea was written large across my face: blazoned there in awe at the sheer audacity of my thinkings. I could hardly pronounce the words.

'We've done many marvellous things,' he said, encouragingly. 'I daresay we could manage one more.'

Poor fool. He imagined I had something sensible in mind, something halfway achievable, and I wondered where he had got that idea. 'Orlando's got another couple of regulators ready,' I said in a rush. 'If we're taking everyone down there anyway—Milady's committed us already—well, what if we could—what if we could—'

'Just say it, Ves,' said Jay, his patience expiring.

'What if we could—fix it?'

Jay's brows rose. 'Fix it? Fix Farringale?'

'Yes. What if we could—sort it out. Mend the magickal surges. Get rid of the ortherex. Fix it. And then the Court could send all the might of the trolls out there, and wipe Ancestria Magicka off the face of Farringale forever.'

Jay stared. 'I hardly dare ask, but... do you have an actual plan? Something workable?'

'Well—no, not exactly, but I'm stronger than I used to be, and I think Merlin's powers might be able to accomplish quite a bit. And we've got the regulators now, and Baroness Tremayne to help us—she's Morgan after all, there must be something she could do that would help—and—'

'Yes.' Jay's eyes were very wide. 'We cannot just barrel in there and take on the entire mess that is Farringale without having a solid plan. No!' he said, when I tried to interject. 'We aren't winging this. It's crazy.'

'It's crazy,' I agreed. 'Wonderfully, superbly crazy. Don't you trust me?'

'To—to take on centuries of disease, neglect and decay at the age-old capital of the troll kingdoms more or less single-handedly, in the face of serious opposition from Ancestria Magicka, and without any clear idea what you're going to do? Am I supposed to have a ready answer to that?'

'You're supposed to say "yes".'

Jay passed a hand over his face, as though to clear the mist from before his eyes. 'You know, the craziest thing is that I probably do. But I shouldn't.'

'Come on, Jay! Imagine how incredible it will be if we can pull this off.'

'I'm imagining how much of a disaster it will be if we can't.'

'It could be a disaster if we don't,' I returned, grimly. 'We're sitting here talking, while Fenella Beaumont and her horrible friends are looting the libraries, enslaving the griffins, and conducting who knows what other nefarious activities within its unprotected borders. We've got to do something.'

'We are doing something. This entire council is for the doing of *something*.'

'And that's wonderful, but it is also *slow*.'

We had attracted Alban's attention with our whispering. 'Ves,' he said, leaning over. 'Is this true? You've got a way to make the site safe for us?'

'No,' said Jay.

'Maybe.' said I. 'I could try—'

'That would change—everything.' Alban stood up, and went away to confer with his royal parents—leaving me to face Jay's wrath alone.

And he was wroth with me. 'Ves, this isn't just a you-and-me adventure anymore. This is serious. The stakes couldn't be higher. Don't make promises to these people when you can't keep them!'

I could have protested that I hadn't promised; I'd only said I could try. But that would be quibbling. Jay was right: I'd raised an expectation and now I had to find a way to fulfil it. 'What's the worst that could happen?' I said instead. 'We try and we don't succeed, leaving us no worse off than we are now.'

'The worst that could happen,' answered Jay, with that terrible, elaborate patience he gets when he's entirely at his wit's end with me, 'is that we wreak some fresh disaster upon Farringale, unleashing unknowable but doubtless appalling havoc upon a city already sorely beleaguered, and emphatically make things *worse*.'

'That isn't likely.'

'It's a more likely outcome than success.'

Jay, I knew, was no risk taker. He was steady and me-thodical; he liked to feel fully in control, to know exactly what to do and what to expect. That he put up with me at all was a source of wonder to me; when I asked him to take a leap of faith on my account, and barrel down the road of recklessness in *hope* of a good outcome, I asked a great deal.

I'd never asked more of him than I was asking right then. I took a deep breath. 'Jay,' I said, very seriously. 'Will you trust me? This one last time?'

'It won't be the last time.'

'I'll never ask anything this crazy of you again.'

He pointed a finger at my face. 'That is a promise you definitely can't keep.'

I tried a smile. 'How many lost and devastated cities can I possibly find to test my powers upon?' A moment's thought forced me to add, hastily, 'Don't answer that.'

His mouth twitched: a smile, ruthlessly suppressed. 'I'll make a bargain with you.'

'Yes!' I said, elated. 'I agree.'

'You haven't heard my terms.'

'I trust you. I agree to any terms you name.'

He eyed me. 'You can't do this alone, and I absolutely decline to try it as your sole support. Thus. If Milady—*Queen Mab* herself—is in favour of this insane scheme, then I'll go along with it.'

I clutched at Jay's arm in delight. 'Yes. Thank you. I know she'll want us to try.'

'Do you know that?'

'Yes,' I said, a bare-faced lie.

Jay, finally, grinned. 'You've got your mother *and* Mab to convince; you'd better get cracking.'

I looked over at Alban, still in conference with the king and queen, along with a severe-looking Yllanfalen lady and a pair of trolls I didn't know. He gestured at me, and several pairs of eyes fixed upon my tentatively smiling face with clear intent. Whether I liked it or not, I'd convinced *them*; I could only hope that I hadn't finally, irrevocably, bitten off far more than I could chew.

10

THE MEETING DIDN'T CLOSE so much as peter out, dissolving into ragged knots of people promising aid and plotting tactics.

Jay and I were called on to describe the situation in Farringale, and to express the Society's intentions regarding its resolution. Once done, our part was largely finished. Alban excused us, and escorted us out.

'Our regards to Milady,' he told us outside the great meeting hall, evidently about to zip off somewhere.

'You mean Mab,' I said, spurred by some spirit of mischief.

An odd look crossed his handsome face: the sort that spoke of indecision. To dissemble, or not to dissemble?

'You knew, didn't you?' I accused. 'The Court's known forever, probably.'

'I did know about Milady's identity,' he admitted. 'I was asked to keep it to myself.'

I fumed a bit, though silently. I could hardly blame Alban for keeping his sworn word, and it wasn't his fault that Milady had never decided to trust *us* with the knowledge.

'She had her reasons,' he said, gently enough.

I sighed. Of course she did, and if I could put aside my own feelings for a moment, I could take a guess at hers. Knowing some part of the truth about Milady changed things, there was no question about that. I'd known her – sort of – for over a decade, and yet, now that I knew her to be *Queen Mab*, my impression of her was markedly different. She hadn't ceased to be the solid, wise, reliable chief of our odd little organisation, exactly; she was still that. But she was something much larger, too.

And I hadn't known. Hadn't even guessed.

'Everything's changed so much lately,' I said, a little plaintively. 'I can't keep up.'

'Things have changed,' he agreed. 'But some things haven't, and won't.' He winked at me, kissed my cheek and left, with a nod to Jay.

'Which things aren't changing?' I asked Jay.

He took my hand, and squeezed it. 'Most of the things that matter. A few of the things that do, but we'll manage.'

'I like that "we",' I offered, and leaned on him for a moment.

'I'll be here,' he said. 'That isn't changing. Come on. Let's go talk to Queen Mab.'

THE ATMOSPHERE AT HOME proved unusually tense. Jay and I whisked our way back to the henge in the cellar, and stepped smartly up the stairs. We were suffering a fair degree of weariness at that point, after a long day of events; but our dreams (or mine, anyway) of a quiet moment with a cup of chocolate were instantly dashed.

I'd no sooner stepped off the stairs than several people dashed by, almost mowing me down as I emerged. One of them was Melissa, offering a distracted greeting as she bombed past, clearly on a mission. Halfway down the passage towards the kitchens—if I couldn't have a peaceful hour in the first-floor common room, I could at least bother Magnus for a snack—I ran into Zareen, or the other way about.

'Ves! Where've you *been*,' she proclaimed, snagging me by the arm as she passed, and dragging me along with her. 'Everything's gone mad. We're being mobilised. You'd think there was a war on, or something. If anybody knows what it's all about, it'd be you. Is it true that Farringale's under siege? They're saying Milady's some kind of fairy queen? I'm telling you, it's mental.'

Preoccupied with doing my best to keep up with Zareen's frantic pace, I managed no more than a few, vaguely assenting syllables.

They were enough. Zareen stopped dead. 'No. It's all true?'

'More or less,' I said. 'I mean, Farringale isn't exactly under *siege*, but it's certainly under a kind of attack. And Milady—'

'Queen Mab,' Zareen interrupted. 'That's what they're saying, but surely not, that'd be crazy.'

'It's true.' I looked around for Jay, hoping for backup, but he was nowhere in sight. 'You remember Baroness Tremayne?' I caught her up on recent events as we walked—half ran, really—and wondered, idly, where she was taking me. I was too tired to care overmuch. Milady would want me soon enough, and until then, I might as well go along with Zareen.

I did wish Jay hadn't vanished, though.

'That explains a few things,' Zareen said, when I'd finished. 'Miranda's holding some kind of council of war in the convention room. Everyone who's ever so much as looked at a magickal beast is in there with her. And Rob's got half the rest mobilising to mount what he's calling "a firm defence" but it sounds more like it's going to be the bluntly aggressive kind. Ornelle's handing out Wands like she's running a sweet shop, though I don't suppose you need any of that sort of thing now—'

'And where are we going?' I managed to interject, slightly out of breath after two flights of stairs.

'Indira said—' Zareen began, but as she spoke a great bell sounded out of nowhere, tolling three times. It had the deep, sonorous roar of those massive cathedral bells, and it seemed to be coming from everywhere all at once. Zareen and I both stopped dead, and clapped our hands over our ears—not that it did us much good. The tolling vibrated right through to my bones.

In the wake of the third strike of the bell, Milady's voice rolled and echoed through the corridors of the House. 'My dear Society. We find ourselves in a state of emergency, as you are no doubt all aware. I call upon each and every one of you to answer the call of Mandridore, and of Farringale. Those willing to participate in a mission of great urgency and likely danger shall assemble in the great hall immediately.'

'Right.' Zareen changed course, heading for the hall, and I dashed after her. We were going—going now, right now, there would be no more time to prepare. So great was the confusion of my thoughts that I scarcely blinked when my mother appeared around a corner, heading our way, and fell into step beside me.

'Cordelia. Good. Here.' She thrust something at me, which I absently took. Only when my fingers closed around the cool, smooth metal of the thing, and felt its latent buzz of magick, did I understand. She'd brought the moonsilver lyre, the lyre of Ygranyllon, her kingdom. Milady must have requested it: one of those moments of prescience she seemed to have, a hunch that we'd need it.

'Mum?' I said, fuzzily. The lyre was singing to me already, all the deep magick woven into its ancient frame calling to all the magick woven into mine. 'What are you doing here?'

She looked at me like I was a complete idiot, and perhaps I was at that moment. 'I've brought *that*,' she replied, indicating the lyre I was clutching.

'Yes, but—you're the—you could have sent someone else?'

'Could've,' she allowed. 'But I'm going with you.'

'Oh.' Several more questions blossomed in my mind in response—my mother didn't often volunteer herself to clean up other people's messes; what in the world was she doing involving herself with this one?—but I didn't have chance to ask them. We were arriving at the hall, which was bristling with far too many people, and more were arriving every moment. I caught a glimpse of Jay's face, and Indira's, and felt reassured.

The double doors were open, affording me a glimpse of the green and blue spring day beyond. Several large vehicles waited outside, waiting to convey our forces south.

Our forces. It hadn't seemed real, listening to Zareen babble about mass mobilisation of the entire Society. But now I was here, in the thick of it, it felt terribly real. At last, after considerable and varied forms of provocation, Milady had declared a kind of war on Ancestria Magicka. For the crime of looting the priceless heritage of Farringale, they were going to pay.

Milady's voice rolled over the assembled crowd, loud enough to drown out the tense, excited chatter. 'Quiet, please,' she said, sternly, and the noise died instantly. 'For those unaware: Ancestria Magicka, an organisation with which we have long endured an uneasy relationship, has violated the sovereign borders of the city of Farringale and committed several acts of theft and vandalism against it. This is unacceptable.

'The Troll Court of Mandridore has begged our aid in securing the city, and expelling the intruders. You will all have received instructions: follow them. We are not coming home until Farringale is restored to peace and sovereignty.'

'We?' I ventured, and heard the question echoed around me by several other voices.

'We,' repeated Milady, ringingly, and then added, in a softer tone: 'I am coming with you.'

'I must have misheard,' I said to Zareen. 'She can't have said—'

'She did.' Zareen pointed. 'She's here.'

I couldn't see what she meant, at first: only a wall of people crowded near the doors, Jay among them. But a space was clearing there, people drawing back, away from something I couldn't see.

No. Away from *someone*. I don't know if Milady arranged it herself, or someone else did, but a shaft of golden light beamed down from somewhere above, illuminating the diminutive—*very* diminutive—form of a person I'd never seen before.

She stood a foot tall, if that. In fact, she hovered, for at her back fluttered a pair of gossamer wings, a blur of pale colour and light. Her hair was a white cloud about her face; that face both aged and ageless, for she was not, could never have been human.

That, at least, did not surprise me. I had long imagined her as, possibly, troll; the hints of her connections with the Troll Courts, and with Farringale, had been plentiful. But this, I could never have guessed.

Understanding dawned, like a brick to the face. 'Giddy gods,' I breathed. 'She's Mab.' Not Mab in the same way that I was Merlin—a modern avatar of an ancient power. She was older, far older, than I could ever have suspected, for she was Mab herself, the Mab of legend and of myth.

She'd spoken, once, of feelings which had sent her into the heart of our House for comfort, as I had done: *I myself once spent two days complete in this very room, quite alone.* She had been offered her current role, she'd said, and did not know whether to accept.

I, full of my own concerns, had assumed she had meant a role like mine: a role like Merlin. That she was an archetype, like me, and the Baroness Tremayne. But she'd never confirmed that.

She had been speaking of her role as *Milady*. As the Society's leader. Her other role—Mab—was no role at all: just her.

'Giddy gods,' I managed, near prostrated with awe. No wonder she had so many connections—so much rare knowledge—so many *secrets*. 'Zar. Am I dreaming?'

'We all are,' she answered. 'We've been dreaming her dream for years. We're a part of it.'

Milady, with effortless stage presence, held her pose long enough for the rising chatter to peak, and die away again. Then she said, with a soft smile on her ageless face: 'Are we ready, then? Shall we go?'

We were; we went. Our rag-tag band of scholars, scientists, inventors, librarians, and magicians, led by mythical Mab, filed en masse out of the safe world of our beloved Home, and off to something horribly like war.

11

Jay and I were not to go with the main force. Ours was the role of scout: we were to whisk away on the Winds and get back to Farringale well ahead of Milady and the rest of the Society. We left Rob (apparently in field command) organising our colleagues into teams—or, one may as well say, units—and hurried back down into the cellar.

Indira emerged from the crowd as we pushed and apologised our way back to the cellar stairs. 'Here,' she said, thrusting something into my hands; I caught it reflexively, felt rather than saw what it was. Smooth, jellyish spheres, cool to the touch: Orlando's spellware.

'Restoratives?' I asked in hope.

She nodded once. 'And sleep pearls. Don't eat the red ones.' With which words of wisdom, she vanished into the crowd.

I checked the contents of my palms: I had several red ones, and four green ones. I gave two of each to Jay, and pocketed the rest of the spheres in separate pockets: red ones left, green ones right.

Well, one green one; one of them went straight into my mouth. I blessed Indira's forethought as it dissolved on my tongue, tasting of peaches. They're fast-acting: within a minute or two, a lot of my fatigue had receded, and that delicious fizz of energy began racing through my veins. I was bouncing on my toes as we ran down to the henge, bursting with vigour.

'If only it were possible to feel like this all the time,' I mused, as Jay's Winds of the Ways began to swirl through the room.

'Exhausting prospect,' Jay disagreed, absently. 'You'd never sleep again.'

'I'd never need to.' Jay hadn't taken his yet, that I had seen. I hoped he wasn't going to pull a manly manoeuvre, and stubbornly go without. He had to be at least as fatigued as I was, after several trips through the Ways.

There followed a period of scrambling hurry, Jay too tense and focused for conversation. I chose not to distract him, for fear he might fly us into the side of a building, or smear us, pancake-like, up and down the unforgiving face of a cliff.

Once we emerged near Winchester, it was my turn: my job, to get us over the several miles to Farringale as fast as possible. Addie bore both of us proudly, and shot like an arrow through the balmy skies of southern England. The nearer we got, the greater my sense of urgency; all thoughts of Mandridore faded, and of Mab, replaced by a growing disquiet.

We'd been absent from Farringale for too much of the day. The sun remained high, but the afternoon was wearing away, and what had become of the griffins while we'd been mobilising? What of the rest of the city? For there must be some ultimate purpose behind the raiding of the library, and the subduing of the griffins—not to mention the theft and installation of at least one of Orlando's regulators. What if we were too late? We had—*I* had—given away our presence, earlier. They knew their activities there were no longer a secret. If I were Fenella, I'd have accelerated my timeline to warp speed, and got out as fast as possible—before, for example, the Society and the Troll Court could form a devastating alliance (aided by several other magickal communities), and descend upon them in force.

We might arrive to find the city empty, of griffins and anything else of value. Our enemies gone, absconded with innumerable priceless and irreplaceable articles of troll culture and heritage.

Were I to give voice to my real fear, though, it was nothing of the sort. Why bother with the regulators, if the goal was only to rob the city? Why subdue the griffins, and then—rather than taking them out of the city, as I'd have expected—leave them in situ? They would never kill them: griffins were far too valuable. But if they weren't stealing them, what were they doing?

They'd arrived in force—as we were doing. Was that in order to empty the city as fast as possible? Was it merely a question of bringing as many hands as possible, the better to thieve at speed?

Or had they brought so much manpower to Farringale because they were taking over the city?

Such unhappy thoughts kept me silent with mounting worry through the ten-mile flight, conducted at a speed that might, ordinarily, have set my guts churning with exhilarated terror. As we drew near to the bridge, my reverie came to an abrupt end, and with it, my long silence.

The site was no longer deserted. Stationed either side of the bridge, right there in the open, and very obviously armed with Wands, stood a pair of giants, the largest I'd ever seen. Each had a small unit of mixed troops with them: humans side-by-side with, to my very great dismay, several trolls.

'Crap,' I uttered eloquently. 'That's not—good.'

'That,' said Jay, 'is very bad indeed.'

I pulled Addie up, halting our flight. 'They're entrenched. That's a hostile takeover going on down there.'

Jay nodded. He understood the implications: if they were guarding the gate, and so openly, then they were declaring control of the city. This was a shameless, blatant attempt to seize Farringale entirely, and all its contents.

My heart sank to see trolls down there, supporting a cause so flagrantly founded upon greed. But perhaps it wasn't so surprising, after all. The romance of Farringale could seduce the hardest heart; and since, as far as I knew, the Court at Mandridore had not, until today, publicised their own intentions in the direction of their lost enclave, it mightn't have been difficult for Fenella to sway these to her side.

'What do we do?' I asked Jay, momentarily stymied. Milady's plan to surge through the gate en masse, and attempt a quick overthrow of Ancestria Magicka's forces, had suffered a check already. If Fenella had stationed so many on this side of the gate, I was willing to bet many more waited on the other side.

True, our numbers were still superior; hers would be scattered across Farringale, enacting the various parts of her plan. But still. A pitched battle at the gate was not what anyone wanted.

'We need another way in,' Jay decided. 'And fast.'

'There is no other way in,' I protested. 'That's why we've always faffed around with the keys.'

'There must be. Or there must have been, at one time. It's an entire city. They can't have managed with only one way in.'

'You're right, but it's been closed for centuries. Sealed. Those old ways must be long gone, and even if they aren't, how do you propose to find—and unseal—one of them in the next couple of hours?'

'You've got the lyre.'

I had. I was unlikely to forget it, for the thing sang ceaselessly at me at the back of my mind; an alluring, enchanting melody, hard to resist. I was mentally postponing the moment when I would, inevitably, have to take up the beautiful, dangerous instrument, and play it again. The last time I'd done so, the results had been—explosive. Especially for me.

'What do you imagine me able to do with it?' I asked, cautiously.

'I don't know. But you've got the lyre, and you've got all of Merlin's magick. If anybody can find a way in, and fast, it's going to be you.'

In other words: this problem was all mine.

I felt a surge of panic, and suppressed it. No time for that. Farringale needed me; the Society needed me. *Think, Ves.*

Jay, a warm weight at my back, squeezed my waist. 'You can do this,' he said, sensitive, apparently, to the intense pressure my mind was trying to buckle under.

Addie was beginning to tire: unicorns aren't made to hover. I turned her, and bade her fly a slow circle around the environs of Farringale. 'Can you ward us from sight?' I asked Jay. 'I don't want that lot to spot us, yet.'

'Done,' said Jay, and fell silent. I felt a little surge of magick from him, a charm woven around Addie and her riders: if we were visible at all to those below, we'd appear as a large bird.

One problem solved. I let Addie and Jay take over our direction: my mind shifted to the problem of entry.

Jay, broadly, was right: there must have been another way in, once upon a time. Any fae settlement or enclave typically had two ways of entry and egress: one between the enclave and the outside world, and one communicating with the wider dell magickal dell in which it was situated.

The bridge over the river Alre belonged to the former category. What of the latter? Was there a way into Farringale Dell, besides going through Farringale itself?

I fished in my trusty satchel, and withdrew the glorious, glittering lyre. Time was, they'd never have simply handed the thing to me: far too dangerous. Its deep, wild powers were wont to overwhelm me. That they had done so now—my mother, anyway, apparently on Milady's orders—disquieted me rather. Was it that I was powerful enough now to bear it? Or was the threat to Farringale so dire, and so important, that I was considered an acceptable sacrifice?

No. My mother might throw me under the proverbial bus, if it suited her, but Milady wouldn't. I had to trust her judgement—and my own strength. I was, after all, much mightier than I used to be.

I took a breath, and did my best to dismiss such an unhelpful spiral of fear. The lyre, cool in my hands, greeted me with a ripple of its airy strings, and a soft swell of its distinctive Yllanfalen magick. At least one of us was pleased to be working together again.

It wasn't hard to lose myself in it. I began to play, one of the plaintive airs I'd once acquired from Ygranyllon:

the melody didn't matter, it was merely a conduit for the magick.

The effects were neither so intense, nor so terrifying, as when I'd played the lyre in the town of Vale. There, I'd been on another world: a more deeply magickal world than ours. Here, there were no such currents to sweep me away. This was our own plain, stolid Britain, a magickal backwater, and the threads of latent power I was able to perceive, even with the lyre, were meagre indeed.

I closed my eyes as I sank into the spells I was weaving; when I opened them again, an altered landscape lay spread before me. I saw, through Merlin's eyes, a blanket of rolling green, dotted with knots of trees, and the clustered rooftops of towns. Laced through this verdure ran rivulets of ancient magick, latent and weak, half smothered by technology and time, but they held; oh, they held.

And there, away towards the Farringale gate: a savage pull of deep power, like the undertow of the ocean. Farringale lay tucked between the spaces in this landscape, on the other side of its fortified gate; but a city so ancient, so magick-drowned, could not help but exert its influence.

'That way,' I murmured to Addie, and it seemed to me that my voice echoed, throbbing with profound magick—painfully so. The currents shook me to my bones, and on some deep, frightening level I wanted to hurl myself into it—merge with it—drown in that sea of power. I would emerge—changed. Something other.

I gritted my teeth, and focused afresh on Farringale. On the dell I sought, and the way through. My mind skittered across that landscape of leylines, testing, probing, touching—there. There, a concentrated knot of magick, a thousand layers deep. An ancient cluster of charms, dormant now, shuttered like a window against the sun: but they had opened something, once, had presided over the passage of a thousand long-dead souls.

A gate—or what had once been a gate. It would be so again.

'I've got it,' I said.

12

'I DON'T THINK YOU'LL like what I'm going to do with it,' I felt obliged to add, as Jay's face broke into a smile of relief.

The smile vanished. 'All right, break it to me gently.'

'No time.' The sight of so many of Fenella's people guarding the bridge had rattled me. What were they doing in there, that required so heavy a defence? The Society would be arriving any time now—they'd got royal permission to use the old troll roads; they'd be practically flying along—and they needed to be able to get straight in. I didn't have time to negotiate with Jay.

By the time those two terse words left my lips, I was already at work. The gate was entirely defunct—no surprise there. I couldn't tell what had functioned as the portal, long ago; probably a boulder or some other, like object, those were popular choices. Doubtless it had been cleared away when Farringale was sealed up. Nothing remained, then, for me to reawaken, and I had neither the time nor the knowledge necessary to create a fresh new gate here.

But we had encountered a similar problem recently, and I'd solved it. Inadvertently, yes, by way of an involuntary burst of magick I did not immediately know how to replicate. But if I'd done it once I could do it again.

I did as I had then, and sat down, putting the greater part of myself in direct contact with the ancient earth and its faded memory of magick. Not so difficult, really, to imagine myself a part of it; to lose myself in the peaceful sway of verdure, the soft and sharp smells of loam and sap; to join the dulcet notes of my lyre and my magick to those lacing the landscape around me. I heard, and felt, Jay shift beside me: an attempt to stop me, hastily suppressed. He would guess what I proposed to do, wouldn't like it; would nonetheless accept, as I had, that the need was great and options few. I felt a stab of compunction as he settled again, and I turned my attention from him: how often had I cast him into torments of worry on my behalf? How often had I outraged his sense of caution, worn out his patience, ignored his fears—*I'm sorry, Jay,* I thought distantly, but I couldn't say so, couldn't even think about it right then, for I was shifting—bleeding into the landscape bit by bit—soon I was scarcely Ves any longer, naught left of me but a stray wisp of awareness, like a dream fraying away upon the wind.

IT HAPPENED FAST. TOO fast. One minute she was Ves, seated at my feet, smiling apologetically at me with that damned lyre in her lap and magick wreathing round her like moths to a flame—and then she was gone, and there sat a Ves-sized rock, a craggy old boulder that looked for all the world as though it had been there since the dawn of time.

No ordinary boulder, of course. This one had motes of a purplish crystal laced through it, with flecks of silver—and, incidentally to its appearance, a profound magick about it, as old as Farringale itself (apparently) and very much functional.

'A Fairy Stone,' I sighed, and felt a stab of pain lance through my temples: a migraine on the approach. Perfect.

'Okay,' I said, and laid a hand against the cool, rough stone where Ves's head had so recently been. 'It's okay. I'll get you out of this—later.'

The incident with the chair, not to mention the tree, had proved all too clearly that the risks of Ves's latest methods remained considerable. She could get herself into these messes; she needed me—us—to get her out of them again.

Later. She'd done this for good reason, and the next part was my task.

I called the number Milady—Mab—had recently given me, for just this purpose. She answered in seconds. 'Jay?'

'We've got a way in,' I said without preamble. 'She's done it. I'm sending you co-ordinates.'

'Thank you.' Brief words, but a world of relief lay behind them.

'Hurry,' I said. 'And avoid the main gate. It's heavily guarded. Don't let them see you.'

Nothing to do, then, but wait: and worry. About the progress of Ancestria Magicka's plans, inside Farringale where they were, for the moment, unopposed. About my colleagues at the Society, about to face a unique challenge we may or may not be truly prepared for.

Most of all, about Ves, inert at my feet, so bound up in her myriad magicks that she might not, this time, ever get out of them again.

Not the most tranquil hour of my life.

Time moved agonisingly slowly, but Milady, thankfully, didn't. I heard sounds of approach, and tensed, alert, heart pounding—ready to defend Ves and Farringale both to the limits of my ability—but it was Rob, striding over the heath towards me looking grim as death, and around him some twelve or fifteen of our colleagues. He'd trained every one of them, I knew: they were the best of us at the *direct arts*. By any other name, fighting. The advance force. Of course they'd be going in first.

Rob nodded at me, and looked around, nonplussed. Expecting to see either Ves or something that obviously looked like a gate, if not both.

I indicated the Fairy Stone, and Rob stared at it, frowning. 'Ves hasn't gone in alone, has she? She's extremely competent but it's far too dangerous—'

'That's Ves,' I said. 'She's the gate.'

Rob was silent a moment, and then said: 'You seem to be taking it well.'

'It does seem that way, doesn't it?' I answered tightly.

He gave me another terse nod, this one tinged with sympathy. 'We'll be quick.'

And then he was gone, one hand planted firmly atop the stone-that-was-Ves, once. Magick surged as the members of his unit went in after him, one after another in a steady stream. By the time they were through, another group were arriving, and streaming into Farringale; faces blurred together as they went by me, too many to note, and I wondered whether it hurt Ves, whether she was even aware. She was strong, but she'd only done this sort of thing for a few of us before; now for fifty, seventy, a hundred...

Milady was among the last to arrive. Rob was her general, leading the charge: she was the shepherd, keeping everyone together, watching the rear.

She had Miranda with her, which was interesting. Miranda looked pale, tense and resolute. I wondered whether Milady kept her close out of trust, or its opposite, and perhaps she was wondering the same thing.

'Thank you,' Milady said again, to me, just before she went through. 'Dear Ves. I hope she has not overreached herself.'

So strange, still, to look Milady in the face—and such a face; not young, not old, not human—more distinct by its lack, of anything I could call familiar.

Queen Mab indeed; I could have cast myself at her feet, and gladly. 'She has,' I answered. 'She always does. I hope you won't need the gate again, because I'm getting her out of there.'

Milady nodded. 'Follow when you can,' she said. 'I'll have need of you both.'

A grace period for Ves, then, albeit a small one. Good. Had I been ordered to haul her straight into the fray, I wouldn't have been obeying it.

Milady awaited no response. In an instant she was gone, Miranda with her, leaving me alone with the inert lump of stone that was my maddening, alarming, adored and magnificent Ves.

I crouched down by her, set a careful hand to her lichen-covered surface, and spoke low and soothingly. She would be suffering, right about now. 'I'm going through. And then we're done. Okay? Just a couple more minutes and we'll get you out of there.'

No response, of course: I wasn't expecting any, though a faint hope withered and died. One last surge of magick, and magick took me, whirled me away: I entered Farringale Dell.

I looked around, oblivious to the landscape, to the knots of Society agents still in the process of disbursing. My only thought was for Ves: specifically, the appalling and impossible absence of her.

The Fairy Stone was not here.

How was that possible? Surely it could only function as a gate *because* it spanned the gap between the outer world, and the Dell: like a door, or a bridge. It had to be here—*she* had to be here—but it wasn't. She wasn't.

And because the stone wasn't there—the *gate* wasn't there—I couldn't go back through and find her, either.

She was stuck, lost, and I'd lost her.

IT OCCURRED TO ME, distantly and belatedly, that we really ought to have warned Baroness Tremayne before we returned in force.

Not that the thought caused me much alarm. It's difficult to feel distress, as a rock. There's a stolid placidity to stone that one cannot help but absorb, even when one is only *mostly* a rock.

I had forgotten her altogether—Jay, too—everything, really, beyond the perimeter of my own boulder. A peaceful interlude, altogether. But a voice intruded upon my dreaming serenity, an insistent voice that vibrated through the core of me, demanding attention.

Cordelia Vesper, it said, over and over again, and I remembered that was my name.

Yes? I answered, cautiously.

Is that you?

Was I Cordelia? Distantly, I thought so. *Ves,* I answered. *I'm Ves. I think.*

Palpable relief; the voice made some wordless sound, a swiftly expelled breath. A sigh. *Thank goodness. I had thought—there are so many of you.*

I focused, gradually, and remembered. Many of us. Yes. Milady, and the Society, in force. *It's all right. Those are Mab's troops. They're here to help.*

I should have said "we", I suppose, for I, too, was there to be useful. Hopefully. But stone feels no sense of either agency or urgency, and mine were all gone somewhere. I drowsed in a lake of my own magick, lulled and sun-warmed; in seconds, I'd forgotten the baroness again.

Cordelia Vesper, came the voice again, with the insistent note of one who has repeated the same phrase several times, and failed to win a response.

I gave myself a strong mental shake. *Yes! Sorry. I'm Ves.*

We have established that.

Right.

Think you to remain a Fairy Stone all your days?

I thought about that, a bit. Not so terrible a prospect, honestly: quite peaceful. *No?* I ventured.

Your duty is fulfilled, methinks. None now linger about you, save one, at a remove.

One lingered. One! Jay must be the one.

At a remove? What does that mean?

She did not answer me, precisely, only said: *Is it your wish to follow in Mab's train?*

Yes, I said, thinking of Jay more than Mab. I hesitated, struck at last by my predicament: I was a Fairy Stone, and my body seemed to think it had always been a Fairy Stone.

The same problem I'd encountered at Silvessen, not to mention the chair incident. And the tree. How easily my body and mind resigned their customary state, and adopted another's; how difficult it was, afterwards, to think my way back into me.

Ophelia might have some idea as to why, but I didn't. *I'm stuck*, I admitted. I needed Jay, or Zareen, or *somebody*, to pull me out of it again. And Jay was there—at a remove.

Excruciating pain, suddenly: my thoughts dissolved into agony. I felt uprooted, as though grabbed by the hair, and *pulled.*

And I burst out of the stone, the land, the magick, like a weed wrenched out of a vegetable patch—and woke up, screaming, to find Jay's terrified face looming above me.

13

'Yes. Thank goodness—I think? Are you okay? Gods—' Jay was babbling, most unlike him, but he swept me into a fierce hug and somewhere in there I managed to stop screaming.

'I'm okay,' I said thickly against his chest, and I was—mostly. I was feeling an odd mix of profound relief and a strange desolation. For while the baroness had saved me from eternity stuck as a Fairy Stone, she'd also torn me out of the most profound peace I'd ever experienced in my life.

And now here I was, in Farringale, with a lost city to save and a few hundred people embroiled in fervid struggles around us while we did it.

It took me a few deep and tremulous breaths to pull myself together. Jay too, probably.

'Any chance you could stop turning yourself into inanimate objects?' said that gentleman after a while.

'I may not have looked it, but I was fairly animate,' I protested. I'd held a conversation, at least. A bit. Sort of.

'That was not animated. This—*this*—is animated.' Jay grasped both my arms and moved them about, most illustratively. 'I prefer this.'

'Me too,' I sighed, meaning it more than I didn't. I straightened, gently disentangling myself from Jay. 'Right. Where are we at.'

'Farringale Dell,' Jay answered promptly, all business again. He pointed. 'City's that way.'

For once, I didn't even need him to tell me. I could feel it, the deep, irresistible pull of Farringale's wild and roiling magick, a lodestone I couldn't have missed if I'd tried.

I took a proper, long look around, having scarcely noticed my surroundings before. Peaks and valleys, the sort they had in mind when they coined the phrase "rolling hills". Landscape like a rumpled blanket, lusciously green, and—intriguing, this—laced still with that latent sense of ancient power, a tapestry of memory and magick. Would I always be so alive to these things from now on? Or was it the temporary effects of having played the—

'The lyre,' I blurted, rigid with horror. 'I've lost the lyre.'

'At your feet,' said Jay calmingly.

There it was, indeed, and being a magickal object of indescribable power and unimaginable antiquity it wasn't just lying there on its side, patently dropped by a careless hand (mine). It stood tall and proud atop a nicely flattened rock, as though I had placed it there myself with tender care, and it was playing some silent melody to itself: its glittering strings visibly vibrated.

'I'm not sure I should be trusted with any more irreplaceable artefacts,' I decided, though this one seemed to be able to take care of itself. 'Will you carry it?'

Jay picked it up, gingerly, and stood frowning. 'I think,' he said after a moment, 'that you'll have to take it after all.' He held it out to me.

I eyed it doubtfully. It shone at me, enticingly, radiating magick in most tempting fashion; but then it tends to do that. Nothing unusual there.

'It's singing at me,' Jay elaborated.

'And that isn't a good thing.'

'Emphatically not a good thing.' Jay winced as he spoke, as though his teeth hurt.

The fact that I'd dropped it apparently didn't mean that the lyre and I weren't still all tangled up together. I took it from Jay's hands feeling only slightly aggrieved.

It played me a joyous ode, which mollified me—a little. 'Everyone's gone,' I observed, for we were entirely alone on the windswept hillside.

'Gone into the city, and we should follow. Are you ready?'

'Of course not.'

'Me neither.'

Jay set off, striding grimly over hill and dale like a modern-day Heathcliff. Breathless with magick and panic and admiration, I trotted in his wake.

HEADING INTO THE TEETH of that magickal mess was like wading into the ocean against the incoming tide. It beat at me, waves of it, relentless as the sea—and all the while, the sense of irresistible force, an undertow waiting to sweep me up and drown me in it.

If it weren't for Jay just ahead of me, advancing upon it like a human wrecking ball, inflexible as death itself, I might have turned tail and fled like a frightened hare, lyre and all. We could've been happy, me and the Yllanfalen Lyre. In Barbados, possibly, or the Seychelles.

But if Jay could face Farringale, so could I. We could face it together.

We had to.

The gate into Farringale city looked so much like an actual entrance I was almost disappointed. No cunningly disguised rocks or airy archways of subtle magick; this one was obviously and unabashedly a door. A grand one, to be sure: ten feet tall and wrought from solid granite, with a set of double doors occupying an ornately carved frame. They looked like they'd been there since the dawn of time, and hadn't been opened in almost as long.

I wondered how the first teams to reach them had contrived to get them open, but they had: one stood far enough ajar for a human to slip through, if not a troll. I glanced through, and saw nothing but a white mist, like dense fog.

'I'll go first,' said Jay, and went, without even waiting for me to reply.

'Wait—' I began, but too late. He was gone, leaving me alone with the hills and the doors and the lyre and the mist.

'Damnit,' I muttered. Nothing for it. I grabbed what passed for my courage with both hands, and stepped into the fog.

Jay caught me on the other side, physically grabbed me. Presumably before I could manage to wander off and get myself lost (plausible). 'The doors lead right into the centre,' he told me. 'We're near the library.'

Or what was left of it, after Ancestria Magicka and I were finished with it. I blushed a little at the recollection: had I knocked down a wall on my way out? I might very well have.

'Which also means,' he continued, 'we're near the mews where the griffins were being kept.'

I read the unspoken question in there. Now that we'd made it inside, what did we want to do? Milady hadn't assigned us to any particular unit, nor given us any particular task.

I knew why. My not-so-secret personal mission, mad as it was: I'd personally declared war on the ortherex. Milady hadn't endorsed it, but she hadn't forbidden it either. She'd left Jay and I free to choose where we placed ourselves and our talents.

I chose to conclude that a lack of active opposition from Milady was as good as support, as far as Jay's reservations were concerned. And I'd go on thinking so unless and until he clearly stated otherwise.

I chewed a thumbnail, thinking. If I wanted to purge Farringale of its infestation, how would I even do that?

They were feeding off its wild flows of magick, or so we had theorised. It was those surges of power that kept them here, oddly static, like the rest of the city. If I wanted to remove them, I'd have to take away their source of sustenance.

I'd have to take the magick out of Farringale. All of it.

A thought I'd been shying away from ever since the emergency council at Mandridore. It was too insane, even for me; too vast, surely, to be accomplished, even with all the magick of Merlin at my disposal.

I didn't want to consider the possibility that I *couldn't* do it, at all—that it wasn't within my power, or anyone's. Because that would mean accepting defeat. There wasn't a way to save Farringale for the trolls without clearing the ortherex, and as long as they had all the deep power of ages to feed upon, they'd be here forever.

We had to find a way, or give up on Farringale. And I wasn't prepared to do that.

I looked at Jay, and his face told me he knew. He hadn't mentioned the griffins at random. 'We've got to get them out of here, haven't we?'

'Yes,' he said.

The griffins, bound up inextricably with the magickal ebbs and flows of Farringale. The very heart and soul of it, the core; without them, magick would wither and die, and Farringale Dell with it. And they'd been resident here for more centuries than I could imagine.

Taking them out—all of them—I didn't even know what that would do to the city. But I knew that I couldn't perform my nigh-impossible task in the face of all their terrible power.

'Miranda's team went straight there,' Jay said. 'With Rob's. They'll be—I don't know what they'll have done by now.'

'And Indira?' I asked.

'Retrieving the regulators. Plus she's got two more that Orlando rushed.'

Good. We'd be needing those. Four might be... enough. Perhaps.

'Right,' I said. 'Let's go.'

WE PASSED FEW PEOPLE on our way through the contested streets of Farringale, at least at first. The combated areas were elsewhere; nobody had cause to care about the library anymore, not now I'd emptied it of its treasures.

Nonetheless, the atmosphere of the city couldn't be more different from our first visit. A palpable tension set my teeth on edge, a sense of urgency, of menace; and the magick of Farringale tossed and roiled like the sea in a storm. It dizzied me, threatened to overwhelm me—what in the name of all the gods had they *done* with the regulators? Not to mention the griffins—Jay had to steady me several times when I threatened to topple under it.

The lyre wasn't much help. I felt like a tree trapped betwixt two hurricanes, each of them trying to tear me to pieces.

When we neared the griffins' makeshift prison, the fraught peace quickly shattered. I heard a tumult of voices raised in conflict, and a terrible, sharp, raucous cry that could only have come from a griffin. Jay and I quickened our steps down a widening street, passing towering townhouses of brick and stone at a near run.

The mews had become a battleground. We tore into an open square, lined on three sides with large, brick-built stable blocks. I counted four griffins still captured, chained and enchanted, unnaturally placid. People were everywhere, I couldn't tell how many were ours, and how many Ancestria Magicka.

I recognised Fenella Beaumont, however, poised beside her imprisoned griffins like a queen holding court. She was dressed all in black, tight trousers and jacket, with her grey hair tied back: practical attire for taking over a city.

She had a Wand out, something emerald, by the look of it, and she was pointing it at Rob.

Rob, unmoved, had his own Wand trained on her right back. He was flanked by his entire team, but then so was Fenella. We had a stand-off going on.

I looked for Indira, or Zareen, but didn't see them.

'Release the griffins,' Rob was saying, calmly but firmly. 'You are surrounded. Reinforcements are imminent. You cannot win this.'

Fenella looked by no means ready to accept defeat, and I wondered afresh what her plan had actually been. If her only goal had been to empty the library, well, she and her organisation should be long gone by now. They'd have no further reason to stay.

But they'd seized control of the gate, and the griffins. Something else was afoot, something much larger. Surely she hadn't thought she could get away with occupying Farringale?

'We're so close,' Fenella said angrily, which wasn't an answer to anything Rob had said. 'Let us work, Rob Foster. We're doing great things—things the Society can only dream of—'

'Oh, balderdash,' I interrupted, and stepped forward. 'What could you possibly be doing that involves imprisoning the—' I stopped, because as I spoke a horrible thought entered my head.

Fenella's eyes glittered with rage at sight of me. 'Ah, the great Merlin,' she said nastily. '*You* should have joined us when you had the chance.'

I didn't waste any time wondering how she'd heard about my new role: expecting to keep anything much from the knowledge of these sneaks was clearly futile. Ignoring her remark, I said, warily, 'What exactly is it you think you're doing?'

She smirked at me. 'Can't you guess?' And I could guess, of course I could: for weren't the Society and Ancestria Magicka like opposite sides of the same coin? I heard, with a horrible sense of inevitability, the expected words fall from Fenella's smirking lips: 'We're saving Farringale.'

14

'*You're saving Farringale*,' I repeated, with perhaps an unwise emphasis on the first word. I was conscious of a stir around me: a reaction from the assembled Society, but I couldn't turn to gauge what it was. I kept my attention on Fenella.

'Of course,' she said grandly. 'Urgent work, I am sure you must agree. The Court won't thank you for getting in the way of it.'

'Oh? You're here on the authority of Mandridore, are you?'

'Of course,' she said again, to my great surprise. I'd expected hedging, deflection, excuses, but not a bare-faced lie.

For an instant, I wondered if it might be true. The king at Mandridore had tasked us with rehabilitating Farringale, if we could; might they have contracted Ancestria Magicka to do the same? From their perspective, the end goal was important, not the tool they used to achieve it. It was plausible.

But I remembered the patent horror with which the Court had heard the news of Fenella's incursion. The urgency with which they'd appealed for aid. It was possible they *had* employed Ancestria Magicka, and that grubby organisation had betrayed them—but I didn't think so. More likely a lie.

But a believable one. Now I understood how Fenella had recruited trolls to her cause.

'That is untrue,' I said. 'We've just come from Mandridore, and they certainly didn't send you.' Futile, really; my word against hers; their word against ours; people would go on believing whatever they wanted to believe.

Fenella waved this away with visible scorn. 'I suppose you'd like me to believe they sent *you.*'

As though it was so far-fetched a possibility, considering she'd called me *Merlin* herself. 'What's your plan?' I said, tiring of the tit-for-tat.

Fenella, off-balance, blinked at me. 'What?'

'Your plan. For saving Farringale.' I swept an arm out, indicating the sorry state of the noble griffins, the clusters of her people guarding the mews, and the expanse of our people ranged in opposition. 'This is all part of it, I suppose?'

I was curious to see whether the whole story was a lie; the "saving Farringale" a story spun to justify the looting, the thieving. Or was there some truth to it after all?

'I'm sure *you* don't need me to explain it to you,' she answered, which was a cop-out, but also true. I didn't.

I was looking at everything they'd done in Farringale with fresh eyes. What they'd done to the griffins.

If we—I—wanted to restore Farringale, we had to neutralise its wild magick, which meant neutralising—temporarily—the griffins. Is that what they were doing?

And what of the library? Had they been looting it, or extracting it prior to potentially damaging magickal procedures?

They'd stolen our regulators from Silvessen, but not, apparently, to sell them, or even to copy them (though I'd be willing to bet they'd be doing the latter at some point). They'd brought them here, to Farringale, and—used them. Hmm.

'And what happens once you've saved it?' That was Jay, his tone ringingly sceptical. 'Who gets control of it?'

'Why, Mandridore, of course,' said Fenella, sweetly.

I sighed, frustrated. It might have been true; it wasn't hard to imagine the kind of fame and favour they could win by such a feat. The Troll Court would owe them for generations.

It might have been a lie, too; I wouldn't put it past Fenella to covet a small kingdom of her own, given half a chance.

We had no way of knowing, and we were wasting time arguing about it. I opened my mouth to say—I don't even know what, I was running out of ways to counter such slippery insincerity from Fenella—but at that moment Milady materialised, as if from nowhere (and, being Mab, she might have).

Her abrupt appearance caused a fresh stir, on both sides—and stopped Fenella cold. It helped that she was laying it on rather thick, hovering at near eye level with the proud leader of Ancestria Magicka, her wings a glittering blur. She shimmered with myth and magick, a palpable power beyond anything most of us had ever experienced. She inspired the purest awe—and, I hoped, a modicum of fear.

For the first time, I detected uncertainty in Fenella's face. She knew a great many things she shouldn't have, but she had not discovered this secret.

Milady spoke, and her voice rang with all the power and majesty of a legendary queen. 'Fenella Beaumont.' The syllables rolled and echoed, like suppressed thunder. 'This is not your task to perform.'

Fenella straightened her spine, lifted her chin, and stared right back at Mab. 'I say the task belongs to anyone who can perform it successfully.'

'And can you?'

'Yes,' said Fenella, without hesitation. Bravado? Or did she truly have a workable method?

A pause. Then Milady spoke—Milady again, not Mab; those low, calm, soothing tones I'd heard so often at the top of the tower at Home. 'In that case, you will agree to a co-operation pact.'

'We require no assistance,' said Fenella, instantly, and with scorn.

'You may enjoy our assistance or endure our opposition,' replied Milady coolly. 'You will, of course, make the wisest decision.'

I wanted to object. They were not to be trusted; they had not honour enough to keep to their promises. They would pretend cooperation, and then betray us at the first opportunity.

I needn't have worried, however. Fenella had not the wisdom Milady credited her with, nor the guile I'd expected. 'There will be no cooperation,' she declared. 'Farringale is in safe hands. Ours.'

Another pause. This was not the response Milady had expected; she did not have an immediate answer to offer. Tension built; Rob and his team shifted, gathering themselves, preparing to oppose Fenella with force, if necessary.

A terrible prospect, and one Milady had always dedicated herself to avoiding. The Society did not cut swathes through our opponents, maiming at will; we certainly did not kill.

But we could not simply walk away, and leave Farringale in their hands. Theirs were not safe hands; never that. If they would not work with us, then we would have to remove them—by any means possible.

Rob lifted his Lazuli Wand, letting Fenella see it. He was legendarily fearsome with it. 'Release the griffins,' he said, deadly quiet.

Fenella levelled her own Wand at him, stared defiance. Giddy gods, had she such unshakeable faith in the might of her own people? Or was this foolish recklessness, an inability to admit herself bested?

Was she bested? I felt a creeping sense of unease, felt it radiating from Jay beside me. We didn't know the extent of either her forces or the powers they mustered between them. We'd seen giants at the bridge, and trolls; we knew she had the likes of Katalin Pataki and George Mercer at her disposal. As to what, or who, else... we were woefully underinformed.

What if *we* were the ones outmatched, and unable to see it?

'Stop,' I blurted. 'Please. Wait.'

Everyone looked at me. The combined weight of so many surprised, shocked, wondering, tense, frightened, enraged gazes made me shrink, for a moment, bowed under the combined pressure.

And it made it so much harder to continue. Milady wasn't going to like what I had in mind; the glimmers of a plan so risky I felt nauseated from the strain of it.

But it was that, or—disaster.

'You're right,' I said to Fenella. 'The important thing is that Farringale is saved, and if you've got a surefire way to do that then you should go ahead and do it.' I was babbling a bit, not at my most eloquent by a long shot: but I was committed now, and rushed on. 'I expect you'll be wanting to take the griffins out of here, and we won't oppose you, but as a gesture of good faith we would like to offer you the assistance of one of our best agents. She's a world expert on the care and handling of magickal beasts, including mythical ones, and will assist you very creditably in keeping them safe and well.'

There, let her refuse that without losing face. She could hardly reject my offer, not without undermining her own claim to be "safe hands" for Farringale—and the griffins. I couldn't see Miranda in the crowd, but knew she must be somewhere nearby. She'd stay as close to the beleaguered griffins as she could.

Jay was silent at my side, rigid with tension and (probably) anger. He wasn't questioning me, he wouldn't undermine me in front of Fenella. But he had, must have, grave doubts. I could only hope he—and Milady—would trust me.

I could only hope I deserved to be trusted.

Fenella took several long, terrible moments to consider my proposal, and I couldn't breathe for fear that she would decline, this too—or that my own people would break, that Milady would publicly overrule me.

'Very well,' said Fenella, though the questioning look she cast at Milady showed how well she understood the limits of my authority.

I waited in fresh agonies for Milady's response. Would she trust me this time? Could she? What I asked required a huge leap of faith, and I couldn't explain *why*—

'Stand down, Society,' said Milady, softly, and I could almost have wept with relief—and panic.

We were committed. Now I had to make it work.

Miranda went past me, heading straight for the griffins, now she had official leave—directing at me a tense, questioning look en route. I met that gaze squarely, trying, probably futilely, to telegraph reams of thoughts with a mere glance: *keep the griffins safe. Stay close to them. Tell us exactly where they're being taken.*

I knew she would perform the first two without question, but the latter? I was gambling on Miranda, too, on the chance that her confused loyalties had settled: that she was a Society agent again, through and through.

Nothing in her face told me whether or not I was right to put faith in her. Time would tell.

A great deal happened after that, and quickly. Milady mustered our people, and pulled them back; Fenella consolidated hers around the griffins, now surrendered into her dubious care.

Jay bristled with something: either rage or fear, I couldn't tell. I followed him over to Milady, and Rob, and about thirty other Society agents all staring at me like I must be crazy. Or a traitor.

We fell all the way back, leaving the mews to Ancestria Magicka, and regrouped at a safe distance. Handsome townhouses rose on either side of me, looming in judgement, empty windows staring out of stuccoed facades.

'Well?' said Milady.

Jay, beside me, didn't move, or barely so. But he'd stopped very close to me: his arm pressed against mine, a reassuring pressure. He might think I was crazy, but he was standing beside me anyway.

My courage rose.

'The thing is,' I began. 'She's right. Someone's got to save Farringale. We can't just leave it like this, and now we have the technology to—'

'Our objective in coming,' interjected Milady, severely, 'Was to eject Ancestria Magicka, and reverse any damage they may have caused. That is all.'

'I know, but we can't do that without a fight, a very damaging one, which nobody wants, and we might be—*we* might be the ones driven out. But if the griffins aren't here—'

Rob said, in a voice of controlled anger, 'Ves, the griffins *are not safe* in Fenella Beaumont's hands. She'll never return them. You cannot conceive how priceless they are—'

'I know, which is why I sent Miranda with them. She'll see to their safety and make sure we know how to get them back, later. We didn't come prepared to remove them, but they did, so it's actually quite perfect. And in the meantime—'

'Later? She could take them away and kill them and there would *be* no later—'

'She won't. Not when they're so *priceless*. Please, Rob. I'm going to need your help.'

He eyed me with a look of frank disbelief, a boundless exasperation, and my heart sank.

Milady hadn't relented either, and I couldn't blame her. At last she said, 'Ves. Are you certain you can do this?'

I was silent for a second, in consternation, the full enormity of what I proposed to do settling over me like a leaden cloak. Was I sure? Truly?

'With the right help,' I said, mustering my courage. 'Yes, I think I can.'

Milady nodded once, and that was it. We were committed. *I* was committed.

Giddy gods. What had I done?

15

'You will need the regulators,' said Milady, unruffled now, and resolute. Magick shone in her green gaze as she looked at me, and I wondered. Had she had one of her hunches about this? Some prophetic dream? In the midst of everyone else's surprise—or horror—Milady had been an ocean of mildly disapproving calm.

But then, so was she always.

'They've got one in there with the griffins,' Jay pointed out. 'Indira's got two with her and I hope they've secured the other one Ancestria Magicka stole. Can you manage with three?'

I have no idea was the honest response, but there was no room to be feeble-minded now. 'Yes,' I said stoutly.

Jay, more sensibly, said: 'Well, if we can't do it with three then I don't suppose we can do it with four, either,' and he wasn't wrong.

'Where's Indira?' I said. I felt a terrible sense of urgency, of time rushing past and events spiralling more out of our control by the minute. As soon as the griffins were out of Farringale, we had to be ready to act. Fenella wouldn't leave us much time, not when it became apparent that we weren't going to simply walk away and leave her to it.

'I don't know,' said Jay, tersely.

'She is at the bridge,' said Milady serenely.

How did she know? I saw the question unfurl across Jay's face, but he didn't ask it, and neither did I. Mab had her ways.

'The same bridge that was guarded by several giants and trolls?' Jay said instead, concern replacing curiosity.

'She is well,' said Milady. 'And I believe she has—'

The ground shifted underfoot, and buckled; for a dizzying instant, the world spun, shimmering like a wave of heat. Milady gasped, and crumpled. I tried to run to her side, but the street tipped sideways and fell on me.

When I opened my eyes again I saw Jay's face outlined against the clear sky, grim and silent.

'What happened,' I croaked.

'You and Milady fell. I don't know why.'

I sat up, clutching at Jay. Waves of magick, pure and deep and wild, pulsed through the ground underfoot, each striking me like an electric shock. 'It's a surge,' I gasped. 'But different. Much—worse.'

'It only seems to be affecting you and Milady,' Jay said. 'Or, mostly. I'm not feeling very much—'

'Mab is a being of pure magick,' I said, choking on the stuff as I spoke. I attempted to climb Jay like a tree, the better to regain my feet; he grasped my arms, and helped me up.

'Apparently, so are you,' he observed, steadying me.

'No, but—close to it.' That, I thought, was the problem: I had so much magick woven through my being that I couldn't help but be deeply affected. I felt stirred like a bowl of porridge—whisked like a bucket of eggs—Gods, I could hardly form a coherent thought.

'The griffins are gone,' gasped Milady, both her hands pressed palm-flat against the earth of Farringale, and her eyes alight with its magick.

'Already,' I breathed. 'I thought we'd have more time—'

'Ves,' said Rob urgently, and there was a world of meaning in the word, the tone. *You need to move*, it said. *Now.*

He was right. My Society had trusted me. Farringale needed me. I couldn't let them down.

I felt a moment's sharp regret for the griffins, and smothered it. I didn't have time to worry about them now. That was Miranda's task. I had to focus on mine.

But first, I needed to clear my swimming head.

I considered the lyre, and discarded the idea. Not yet. Not now. Instead I dug out my syrinx pipes, and blew a piercing, jagged trio of notes upon them. The harsh sounds split the air in a discordant jangle, carrying my message to Adeline. *Help. Help me.*

'We need Indira,' I said, fighting to keep my voice steady. 'We need Baroness Tremayne. And we need every regulator that's available. If that's three—two—so be it.'

The surge was still building; we had a little time. But not much. As soon as it ebbed, I needed to be ready.

The air split, and Baroness Tremayne stepped out of nothing. 'I am here.'

'I'll need your—shape-shifting,' I told her. 'Soon.' Conceding the griffins to Fenella's care left me with a problem. If we weren't the ones who had taken them out, then we couldn't decide when to bring them back, either.

The baroness asked no questions, merely nodded her assent, and vanished again. I hoped—trusted—she would stay close, somewhere beyond my perception.

'We need all the regulators,' Rob said. 'Whether you use them or not, Ves, they can't be left in Fenella's hands.'

Right. She'd be trying to use them herself. I mentally heaped curses on Fenella Beaumont's head.

'She'll have taken one of them with her,' Jay warned.

He was right about that. The shifting of that regulator, and the removal of the griffins, had probably caused—or at least were contributing to—the surge. 'One problem at a time,' I said. 'We'll have to—immobilise her. Later.'

And here came Addie, arrowing down out of the sky in a burst of light. She landed heavily, kicking up a spray of earth, and came for me at a gallop. I grabbed for her, hauled myself onto her back; as soon as my fingers touched the soft velvet of her hide I began to feel better. She balanced me, settled the sickening swirl of magick, and my head cleared. I'd still like a sunny afternoon at the grove for optimum results, but it would do.

'Right,' I said, straightening my back. Everything in me ached, like my bones were on fire. 'Time to work.'

I expected words from Milady, instructions, orders, but she lay prone still, like a fallen flower. She would recover—when Farringale did.

Rob was looking at me, expectant. So was Jay, and Melissa, and—everyone.

I swallowed panic, and thought furiously. They were waiting for orders—from me. Right, then. 'A few people need to stay with Mab. If you can safely get her out of here, do so. Jay, with me. We're making a run for Indira. Rob and team: see if you can secure the missing regulator from Fenella. If not, please obstruct her by any reasonably fair, mostly non-violent means available. I need space to do this.'

'Reasonably fair,' Rob said, and nodded.

'*Mostly* non-violent,' added Melissa, and smiled, not at all nicely. I didn't pursue the point. No one would be shedding tears if Fenella emerged with a bruise or two.

Jay swung himself up behind me, like a pro. The days when he'd shied away from riding horseback seemed a long time ago, and I suppose they were. 'Right,' I said. 'Which way to the bridge?'

Jay pointed, and we were off, Addie's hoofbeats thundering against the dry earth like the drums of war.

AT THE BRIDGE, CHAOS reigned. We came barrelling around a corner at a ground-eating canter and nearly ran into the prone form of one of the giants; Addie jinked around the obstacle at the last moment, the abrupt movement nearly hurling Jay off her back. The giant's thunderous snores proclaimed him asleep, not unconscious, and I remembered the last time I'd seen Indira: she'd pressed several of Orlando's sleep capsules into my hands. I still had them.

Indira had put hers to good use, for several other bodies, still as corpses, littered the narrowing white street. Some kind of pitched battle had taken place for control of the gate, but we'd missed most of it. There were people everywhere, spread across the street in a disorganised, struggling mass.

I couldn't immediately tell who was winning, and for a moment everybody seemed a faceless stranger; I recognised none of the people I saw. My heart sank. Were we too late?

Then Zareen came surging out of a knot of people at a dead run, heading for... oh no, that was George Mercer, face set in a rictus of angry determination, Wand raised—for a horrible instant I felt a stab of fear straight to the heart: Zareen wasn't—she *wouldn't*—

No, of course she wouldn't. Miranda had made me paranoid. Nothing in Zar's face registered a welcome—in fact she looked angrier than I've ever *seen*, ready to tear his face off with her fingernails—it took me a second to realise *why*—and I was too late, we were both too late, for Mercer made a smashing motion with his fist, his Sardonyx Wand catching the light in a black slash, and with a shattering *boom* the earth exploded.

A massive spray of earth and stone soared sky-wards—cries of pain rent the air as the dislodged paving stones hurtled down again, striking friend and foe alike.

And something else went flying into the sky—something that glinted eerily silver, flashing like a falling star.

The regulator.

Mercer, in a shattering display of bullish brute force, had blasted the thing right out of the earth. He needed only to catch it, and run...

But Zareen knew George Mercer, and she'd seen it coming. If I'd thought she'd been planning to attack him, I was wrong: with a gravity-defying leap, she snatched the regulator out of the sky, and collided heavily with him on the way down. They fell in a tangle of dirt and stone and limbs but Zar was up again in seconds, ruthlessly smashing Mercer's face into the earth as she went.

'VES!' she yelled. I thought she'd pitch the regulator at me, but she didn't trust it to the skies again. She tore towards us on foot, dodging felled and sleeping trolls, piles of shattered stones and three unwise people who attempted to intercept.

I spurred Addie forward and we galloped to meet her, clearing a snoring giant in one flying leap.

Too late—Mercer was up—however fast Zareen could run, he was faster. He'd be on her before she could reach us.

With a snarl of pure fury, Zareen threw herself forward in a perfect and utterly reckless rugby tackle. She fell heavily, with a sharp cry of pain—but cool metal stung my fingers, and my hand closed on intricately-worked argent.

'Get it out of here!' she roared, looking ready to tear *my* face off if I didn't obey.

No fear of that. 'Up!' I ordered, kicking at Addie's flanks, and we were airborne, winging away from the carnage at the gate with the regulator securely clutched in my fist.

'That woman must've been a terror on the lacrosse pitch,' I gasped, half winded.

'Indira!' Jay shouted in my ear, pointing. 'There.'

The distant shape could have been a bird—I'd have taken it for such—but I trusted Jay. And he was right: the dark blur was bombing towards us at reckless speed, and soon gained a more distinct shape. Indira, *not* demonstrating improbable powers of flight, however it may appear, but seated rather precariously atop a witched slab of something stony, and hurtling our way.

'What the bloody hell—' yelled Jay in my ear. 'She'll *fall.*'

She looked like she might, any second, and she was far too high up. If she fell, she'd die.

'Right,' I said, and spurred Addie on to lightning speed. We had to catch her—now.

16

IT WAS A CLOSE-RUN thing. As we drew nearer, I could see the way Indira wobbled as she sat, the currents of wind knocking her about like a stray leaf.

No time to think. We swooped, Addie's broad wings battling a gust of wind as she banked and turned. Jay leaned—grabbed—he had her; and away we went, spiralling downwards. Strong as she was, Addie couldn't carry three of us for more than a few minutes; we had to get her hooves on the ground, and quickly.

'Thanks,' gasped Indira, breathless.

'What the hell—' said Jay, breaking off abruptly as Addie thudded into a heavy landing. We'd come down in a street I didn't recognise, almost too narrow for Addie's wingspan. Tall, stone-built houses rose on either side, as empty and dead as the rest of Farringale, their small, square gardens riotously overgrown.

'Surge,' Indira said to her brother as she slipped lightly down. 'Boosted me higher than I meant to go, and then the wind caught me.' She made a *whoosh* gesture with one hand, most illustrative.

Jay made no reply, it being a bit late for such niceties as "you should be more careful."

'We were looking for you,' I said, choosing not to get down from Addie's back just yet. The surge roiled on, stirring all the magick in me into a dizzying whirlpool, and I was beginning to feel nauseated.

But that was a good thing; it meant we weren't too late.

'I was looking for you, too,' Indira answered, and produced, from one of her air-pockets, two regulators.

No. I took a second look: three lay nestled in her palm, winking starry silver in the sunlight.

'Rob got the one from the griffins!' I guessed.

Indira nodded. 'Couldn't find you, but he found me.'

I handed mine to her, completing the quartet. Four of them. Would it be enough?

It would have to be. And to echo Jay: what we couldn't accomplish with four, we probably couldn't accomplish with five either.

'Right,' I said. 'It's time.' I tasted bile as I spoke, the product of raw fear. I wasn't ready. I'd never be ready. But if I couldn't make this happen, who else could? Fenella? Improbable, and undesirable besides. Mandridore couldn't be left beholden to such a person as that.

Jay slid down off Addie's back, joining his sister on the ground. But he stayed close, and looked up at me with perfect confidence as he said: 'Where to?'

'The library.' Back to where it all began; where I'd first encountered Baroness Tremayne. Where we'd found Bill, and consequently gained Mauf. The trail had begun there: those first clues leading us from Farringale to Mandridore and all the way to another Britain entirely. It was fitting that our journey would end there, too.

Jay set off unerringly, leading us in a slow procession up the near-silent street. We were silent, too, sober with the weight of responsibility, dry-mouthed with fear, light-headed with magick. When I tried to speak—some nonsense or other to break the deathly quiet—my words emerged half-strangled, a mere wordless croak.

Jay looked back at me. 'Are you okay?'

We were a bit beyond polite lies, so I went for the truth. 'Nope.'

He nodded. 'We can do this,' he said, and his voice rang with all the conviction I'd forgotten how to feel.

I smiled back, a little. 'Let's hope so.'

IF THE STREETS ABOVE had seemed quiet, the cellars beneath the library were like a tomb.

I didn't have to walk through walls, this time—or be dragged, like a sack of potatoes. Jay found a winding way through the bare-walled chambers—stripped, now, of their precious books—along a narrow passage, and down a cramped, spiralling staircase, and we stepped out into a cool, stone-walled subterranean chamber, empty apart from the three of us, and shrouded in an unearthly silence.

I'd had to leave Addie outside, and was already suffering from the separation. But those walls were sturdy and solid, the stone very cold under my hands as I steadied myself against them.

We needed no light. A pallid, sickly glow emanated from the floor, thrown off by a writhing mass of tiny, hungry parasites. I shuddered at the sight of them, a chill of pure horror rippling down my spine. I knew they wouldn't hurt me—they were devourers of magick and, by preference, trolls. They had no interest in a Cordelia.

Still, to set my feet into that mess of wriggling bodies took more nerve than I thought I possessed. I descended from the stairs very carefully, and paused.

Indira, behind me, made a sound of disgust, and her footsteps stopped on the steps.

'Stay there,' I suggested. 'If you can deploy the regulators from up there, then there's no need to come any farther down.'

Indira accepted this suggestion with obvious gratitude. Jay, though, visibly steeled himself, and waded into the echoing chamber to stand beside me. He waited, steady and calm, solid as the stone walls of the cellar itself.

The surge was dissipating at last, its tide of magick spent. The right moment neared; not yet, but *soon*. I set my lyre down on the bottom step of the stairs, near my feet. It glimmered with a pale light of its own, but a cleaner, comforting glow, and I breathed more easily for it.

'Indira,' I said. 'When it's not surging, Farringale's latent magick runs rather low. Probably because it's been empty for centuries. When it hits its lowest ebb... we need to use that momentum. Keep it going.'

'Going—where?' asked Indira.

'I don't know. Ebbing. Dissipating. I want it as dead as Silvessen in here.'

'You want to strip *all* the magick out of all of Farringale.' Indira spoke in tones of disbelief.

'As close to it as we can get, yes. It's the wild magick that's been sustaining these things. I can't remove them as long as they're still feeding off it.'

'Can you remove them anyway?' Jay asked. 'All of them?'

He meant *how*; by what possible method did I propose to obliterate a city-wide infestation of parasites? I didn't have a clear answer, for him or for me.

'Yes,' I told him anyway. One problem at a time. First, the magick; then, the ortherex.

Indira said nothing more, but set about deploying the first of the regulators. I hoped her silence indicated confidence.

A tremor ran through the walls and the floor underfoot; a soft buzz of magick taking effect. Metal scraped over stone, cracking and grinding, and ceased with a jolt. 'One down,' said Indira.

The air split, shattered, and spat out a tall, bulky figure: too much of both to be the baroness. A male troll, simply dressed in a swallow-tailed coat and pantaloons, his hair bone-white with age. He said nothing, but his presence was imposing enough; Jay was instantly alert.

'Wait,' I asked him, holding up a hand. The gentleman had offered us neither violence nor threat, and a stray memory teased at me...had not Baroness Tremayne spoken of others like herself, a year ago? The long-forgotten guardians of Farringale, lingering like ghosts in the walls, had numbered three.

I bowed to the newcomer, for he bore an air of nobility about him. 'Have you come to help us?' I asked hopefully.

He regarded me levelly. 'Can you in truth rid us of these creatures?'

I wished people would stop asking me that. The word "no" kept trying to pop out in response. 'We are going to try our best to do so,' I managed to say instead.

Another grinding, crunching, teeth-aching sound, and the walls shuddered: the second regulator.

'I will watch over you,' said the guardian. 'Foes abound.'

They did indeed. I was going to thank him, but before I could speak I was wrenched out of the world, soul and body together. The room splintered around me, dissolved into the strange, juddering, shadowy alternate reality that I was beginning to despise. We were between the echoes again, one half-step to the left of the flow of time.

'That's one way of watching over us,' said Jay with a grimace.

I watched Indira, poised to assist, for I didn't think she had experienced this particular strangeness before. But she was absorbed in her task, oblivious—or at least, unflappable. A third regulator took effect: one to go.

And the environment was stabilising by the minute, the surge rushing away like the outgoing tide. The regulators were humming, a melodic fizzing in my ears, my bones. 'Jay,' said Indira, his name a summons, a plea, and he went to her.

I left them to it, for they didn't need me for this. I picked up my lyre, and cradled it with momentary tenderness. I think I knew, somewhere in me, what was to come...

'Ves,' said Indira, softly. 'They're in.'

'Good.'

'But—I don't know if you understand. Magick can't just dissipate. It has to go somewhere. There's only so much the regulators can do—'

'I know,' I said. 'It's okay.' I was already turning my mind away from the regulators, from the clever and capable Patels; from the library cellar, writhing with infestation, and from the silent guardian who attended our efforts to save it. I spread my awareness like a net, out through the silent ruin of the library, and down, down, deep into the rock beneath. My fingers plucked a plaintive air from the strings of the argentine lyre, each rich note reverberating through the air, through the floor, through me.

It was worse than stepping into the midst of the ortherex—worse than wading barefoot through the mess and the mass of them. As I opened my mind to the land around me, feeling the cold earthiness of rock and dirt, the clear dampness of groundwater, the bright, surprising freshness of roots winding down from above, I felt the ortherex, too: felt them like a cloak of ants crawling over every inch of my skin. They bit at me, raged at me, a million motes of wrongness and disease.

I shuddered, shaking with the effort to curb my revulsion, to hold my mind down there in that terrible space. There was too much magick, still, swirling in airy currents, like gusts of wind: I could feel it with a startling clarity, the Merlin in me recognising it, welcoming it. The magick was ancient, here; almost as ancient as Merlin himself. It called...

No. This magick was not for me; I was not for it. I was here not to lend it my strength, call it back to all its former potency, but to do the opposite: to dampen it, shutter it, drain it away. Every natural impulse in me rebelled at the idea, and rebelled again: the magick belonged here, deep in the bones of the land, and it was my task—Merlin's task—to protect it. To help it grow.

'I will,' I promised it, distantly. 'Later.'

I bore down with a will, encouraged by the pulse of the regulators around me, my lyre joining with their delicate hum, carolling a dulcet lullaby. If it could not be removed, then perhaps it could be lulled; sink itself down into the bowels of the earth, far below the beleaguered city that was Farringale.

Go, I bade it, and added, pitifully, *please.*

It reacted instead with a surge, a flourishing. It drew me deeper into its flow, made of me a link in its web, a thread in its tapestry of power. More gathered around me, faster and faster; I became a brightening core, a burgeoning nexus of wild magick.

Giddy gods. This was like the lyre, but worse. The magick in me—Merlin's magick—attracted that of Farringale; like spoke to like; I was making it stronger.

A tactical error, I thought with distant hysteria. I'd been wrong. I wasn't the best person for this task, I was the worst; what I had thought to be an advantage proved to be the opposite.

And I was stuck down deep, melded with the sleeping earth below Farringale as magick sank into the very essence of me, and shone.

This was what it was like to be a griffin. Perhaps that had been an error, too; deprived of its foci, the magick of

Farringale had not disappeared, but rather altered in shape, in sense, in current; had seized *me*, their substitute, and would not let me go.

I couldn't fight it. I was strong, but my strength was no asset here: together, we were stronger still, in all the wrong ways.

Well. So.

An alternative idea drifted through my labouring thoughts, and at first I rejected it, utterly and completely. Every cell in me revolted at the notion, strained as I already was. The regulators were beginning to affect me, too, merged as I was with magick: they pulled at me, dragged at me, smothered the spark of my life in thick, grey dullness.

I didn't have much time. I couldn't say what would become of me, under all these competing forces, but I felt frayed like an old blanket, coming apart at the seams. There wouldn't be much of me left, soon.

I searched my sluggish mind for another idea, any idea at all, and found nothing. There wasn't another option.

Focus, Ves. I could bear it—probably. Hopefully.

In the space of a single breath, I stopped resisting the influx of magick, stopped pushing against it, stopped warding myself against the inexorable onslaught. If it wanted me, very well: let it have me. All of it.

I opened myself to it entirely, without barrier, and it came to my call: a vast, onrushing flood of it, drowning me in power—in possibility—in *life*. I had drowned like this once before, in Vale, when I'd first taken up the lyre; but this, *this*, was as the ocean to a lake: unimaginably immense, and far beyond my capacity to contain.

Were it not for the regulators, and the griffins' absence—had I attempted it with the surge at its highest—it would undoubtedly have destroyed me.

As it was, I held it—barely, and briefly; I needed only to focus my attention, frame my intent, fix everything I had upon that other devouring sea, the ortherex.

Power arced about me in a haze of lightning, lethal starfire exploding from the very core of me, setting me alight; I screamed, and screamed again, but it wasn't agony, not quite—

As all the magick of Farringale spiralled and built and blazed around me, I gathered one last surge of will: let it blaze, then, let it burn.

Magick tore through me, and I shattered; into a thousand motes, into a million. A current ripped through Farringale, stronger, far stronger, than even the most potent of its surges: stones thundered and crumbled around me.

And with every pulsing wave that shuddered through the ground, ten thousand ortherex flared with starfire, and winked out.

17

THE PURGING OF FARRINGALE took a long time; time that seemed boundless, endless, in that state, and it seemed to me that I had always been down there among the rocks and roots, a part of the city as ancient, as immoveable, as time itself—and as relentless. I ran through the undercity like a wildfire, like a plague; and when, at long last, I was spent, the city rested in a profound, half-shattered silence.

The infestation was gone. The city had suffered for it, somewhat, but it would stand: time lay spread before it in welcome, bursting with potential, with possibility. The ortherex were a part of its past, now, purged from its present and its future. The people of Farringale could come back.

Great, I thought, weakly; a ghost of something like satisfaction, like joy, passed over my exhausted heart, and faded.

I was spent. I had nothing left, which was good; nothing to draw the magick of Farringale back to me, to keep it about me. I was an echo, a whisper, everything I had once been poured into the earth and stone; and the magick followed, rippling through the city like spreading water. Mine; Merlin's; Farringale's; magick, old and new, sank into the bones of the city and held.

A thought stirred, distantly. *Baroness?* I called, weakly.

Is it time? Came the answer.

Yes.

She withdrew, out of the echoes and into the light. Somewhere above, she would be bringing her own arcane arts to bear, taking on the mantle I had so recently occupied. A griffin would sail the skies over Farringale once more, and all the latent magick of the city would rise up to welcome her.

The rest would return, too, soon enough, and Farringale would be restored in full: its people and its magick, thriving as they always should have done.

Me, though. I was—tired. I was rainwater and dirt, I was weathered stone and the roots of tall trees. I was magick, old and slow, permeating air and brick and rock.

My consciousness faltered, and winked out, snuffed as thoroughly as the parasites I had destroyed. Darkness, thick and serene, enveloped me, and I was gone.

THE EARTHQUAKE LASTED LONG enough to shake Farringale down to its foundations. It ought to have brought the roof down on us; how the walls held I'll never know. The whole world shook in a deafening roar of distressed stone, and all I could do was cling to Indira and pray.

It passed at last, settling into a shocked, hushed silence. Dust and dirt and plaster rained down from the ceiling, centuries of detritus suddenly dislodged. For a time I couldn't see through it—or breathe; we pulled our shirts up to mask our mouths, and choked.

The haze dissolved, bit by bit, until I could see—somewhat. The cellar had gone dark, which, I vaguely realised, was a very good thing. That weird, sickly light was gone, which meant the ortherex were, too. Several long moments passed before my eyes adjusted, and the full impact of what I wasn't seeing hit me.

'Ves?' I called. The word echoed off the blank, bare walls, and no answer came.

Indira summoned a wisp of light with a snap of her fingers. I was already scrambling to my feet, running forward, hoping against all the evidence of my eyes that I'd find her back there. Somewhere. 'Ves!'

'She's not here,' said Indira tightly.

'What do you mean, *not here*. She has to be here.' I looked around wildly, my heart pounding with fresh terror. 'Where else could she possibly *be*?'

Indira looked hard at the neat, square flagstones that covered the floor, and probed at one with the tip of her shoe.

'Gods, no,' I gasped. But it was all too probable, wasn't it, she'd ended up as a stone before—more than once. I might be *standing on her*.

I backed away from where I'd last seen Ves, horrified—and fell over something. My elbow cracked hard against the floor, my head hit the wall, and for a dazed instant I couldn't think.

'That's—' Indira darted towards me, and fell to her knees before a dim object sticking out of the stonework. 'It's—'

'The lyre.' Ves's moonsilver lyre, the beautiful, dangerous instrument we'd unburied from Ygranyllon. I'd never seen it other than luminous, bright silver like the moon, and now it was dead and dark and embedded into the floor of the cellar like it had been there for centuries.

I grabbed it, and tugged uselessly. It didn't budge.

'It's completely inert,' Indira said, wrapping both her clever hands around its frame. 'It's like—normal silver. Like it never had any magick at all.'

Normal silver, swept bare of magick, and grievously tarnished. Its strings were gone; it would never play music again.

'You don't think...' I stared at Indira in horror. 'You don't think the same thing happened to Ves?'

She stared back, appalled. 'That she was—no. Surely not.'

Ves had more in common with Mab than the rest of us, these days: a creature of overwhelming magick. What would happen if something had taken that away? Would she end up like the lyre? Inert. Used up. Dead.

I couldn't think about that for too long. I pushed the thought away, and clung instead to that knowledge of Ves's recent escapades that gave me hope. 'She's just ended up—stuck,' I said, with as much confidence as I could manage. 'Like the Fairy Stone. And the chair.'

'And the tree.'

'Right. We just need to figure out which one she is, and—we can probably snap her out of it.'

Indira and I stared in helpless silence at the wide expanse of the cellar, paved with hundreds of identical stones.

'We're going to need help,' said Indira. 'I don't have anything that... I don't know how to find her.'

I didn't either, but I hated to admit it. Hated to walk away and leave Ves there, even temporarily. Was she aware? Did she know she was stuck? She might be frightened. She'd certainly be exhausted.

'We're coming back,' I said, loudly and firmly. 'Ves? All right? We're coming back for you.'

Nothing answered me, and another shred of hope died. I shook my head, made myself turn my back to the devastated lyre and walk away. We needed to find Milady. She would know what to do. She was *Mab*, magick incarnate.

I hadn't noticed my physical state until I started up the stairs. Then it came crashing in upon me that I'd suffered through an earthquake, not to mention falling and hitting my head afterwards. I had aches and bruises in too many places, and I shambled and staggered up the stairs like an old man of ninety. Indira, spared the embarrassing fall, fared a little better, but she too groaned in protest as we started up the second flight.

When we emerged at last into the open air, breathing in great, gulping gasps, we found a darkening sky. Twilight glimmered overhead, a dim scattering of stars beginning to shimmer. A great, raucous cry split the silence, and a dark shape wheeled overhead, lightning crackling in bursts over its feathered hide.

A griffin. Despite my fear for Ves, something in me smiled, for a moment: magick was coming back to Farringale at last, the way it should always have been.

'She did it,' said Indira, watching the griffin's progress as it banked and wheeled far above. 'She saved Farringale.'

'And now we need to save her. Come on.' I turned away from the griffin's majestic flight, and headed back towards the mews.

It was deserted, empty and still. No sign of Milady, or Rob, so they had moved her after all. But where to? I felt a rising frustration, and choked it down: I had to stay in control. 'The guardian,' I said, suddenly remembering. He had said he would watch over us, but he'd been gone by the time the earthquake had ceased. For a little while I'd forgotten him.

'Let's go,' Indira agreed, and set off at a run for the library once more. I followed with a stifled groan, my abused muscles protesting at the punishing pace.

We clattered back through the streets, clambered over the remains of the wall Ves had bashed her way through when she'd been a tree. In minutes we were back on the stairs. 'Um,' said Indira. 'Did you catch his name?'

I hadn't. 'Baroness Tremayne?' I tried, in case it hadn't been her we had seen in the skies. 'Or—anyone?'

Silence, for three agonising breaths; nothing moved.

Then—

'Yes,' came a voice, a whisper, so faint I could barely hear it. A shape emerged, a wavering outline lightly etched upon the air. Our guardian friend, but—diminished, fighting for breath, bent almost double under the weight of a kind of suffering I couldn't imagine.

'Are you well?' Indira rushed forward to help him, but her outstretched hands passed through empty air.

'I—may be,' he answered weakly. 'In time.'

Time. He had already endured so much of it. 'Is there something we can do to help?' I asked him.

He waved this away, and said, between gasping breaths, 'You seek your—companion.'

'Yes,' I said instantly, hope flaring back to life. 'Is she—can you reach her?'

'She's not—' Indira started, and hesitated over the terrible words. 'She isn't—gone, is she?'

'She remains.' Two little words, but they brought such a world of relief. 'She remains,' he said again, 'but she is... distant. I do not know how to recall her.'

'Can you tell us where Mab is?' I tried. I wasn't sure how I expected him to know, but he was tied into the fabric of Farringale in ways I didn't understand. The baroness knew things, sensed things, that I never could have: would this, her fellow guardian, prove the same?

'Mab,' echoed the guardian. 'Yes. Mab, old as the stones themselves. Her light is—brighter.' He took a breath, steadied himself, and added, 'She lingers at the gate.'

Hoofbeats interrupted anything else he might have said, and a shimmering unicorn came cantering up the street towards us, shining like the very stars and evidently pissed off. She came to an abrupt halt before me, stamped a hoof in pure temper, and snorted.

'I know,' I told her, not daring to touch her when she was in such a rage. 'We don't know where she is either, exactly, but we're working on it.'

'Can you take us to the gate?' Indira said, and was bold enough to approach.

Addie stood quietly as Indira swung herself up, and snorted at me when I didn't.

'Okay, okay,' I sighed, resigning myself to one more bruising, alarming horseback ride, and without the comfort of Ves to hang onto.

She was fast, though, so it was worth it. We left the beleaguered guardian with promises of an imminent return, and thundered through the shadowed streets to the gate.

A small crater made a blank, black hole in the earth, surrounded by debris: the spot where George Mercer had blown the regulator into the sky. Addie skirted easily around it, and came to a halt around the corner, near the elegant archway that marked the gate itself.

A great many people were gathered there, an entire crowd, many talking at once. After the eery quiet of the rest of the city, I found it a relief.

'Mab,' I was already shouting as Addie halted. 'Please, we need Mab. Anybody seen her?'

I was answered, vaguely, in the negative, several utterances in the negative reaching my ears. Milady's voice I did not hear, nor any other that I recognised—

No, that wasn't true. One rose above the others, a raw, somewhat uncouth holler. Out of the milling crowd with a stride like a soldier's came Delia Vesper.

'Jay? Where the bloody hell is my daughter?'

'She's—'

'And what the bloody hell has she been *doing*?'

Delia Vesper had arrived with an entourage. Half the people around her were Yllanfalen, brought, in all probability, from Ygranyllon; they were here to help.

No Mab, though.

'She's in trouble,' I said. 'We know where she is, sort of, but—well, it's tricky to explain—'

'Just spit it out,' she ordered, and I did, pouring the whole story out in a muddled torrent while Ves's mother glared daggers at me.

'Right,' she said when I'd finished. 'Take me there.'

'Can you—'

'Just take me there, and don't talk until we get there. I need to think.'

'I'll keep looking for Mab,' Indira said, making go-forth gestures with her hands.

I went. Addie bore Delia and I back to the library with a kind of boundless energy born, probably, from rage—or fear.

The guardian was nowhere in sight when we clattered once again down the steps, and I didn't call for him again. It had obviously cost him to materialise for us before, and besides, he'd told us all he could. It was down to me, now, and Delia Vesper.

That lady stormed into the cellar like it had personally offended her, and stood in the middle of it, staring wordlessly at the remains of the lyre. 'Right,' she said again, and sat down, her good hand pressed to the cold floor and her other arm draped over the lyre.

That's right: Delia Vesper, the archaeologist (before she became a fairy queen), adept at detecting the lingering traces of past magick. The memory of it, so to speak. I waited in silent hope, hardly daring to breathe, as she did—whatever it was she was doing.

'She is here,' said Delia at last, and opened her eyes in order to glower at me again. 'But it's like she was here ten years ago, not earlier today. What exactly was it you did to her again?'

'Er, nothing,' I blurted. 'Maybe that's the problem, there was something I should have done in order to keep her—ground her, or something—but I didn't know.'

'Right.' Delia tapped a fingernail against the tarnished silver of the lyre, making a tinny, rhythmic, pinging sound. 'The problem is, the person most likely to be able to get her out of there is Ves herself. I don't know anyone else who has the power.'

'We thought Mab—'

'Mab isn't here. I am. And Cordelia is fading fast.'

'Shit,' I said, eloquent as only terror could make me.

'Yes,' Delia agreed. 'I'm going to—'

The air flashed oddly, and fractured—I was starting to hate the way it did that, way too hard on the nerves—and a figure rippled into view: the guardian returned.

No, not the guardian—or, not the one we had spoken to before. Baroness Tremayne. And where her compatriot had been pale and faded, she was all vivid energy and colour. I knew with a sudden certainty that it had been she I'd seen in the twilit skies, revelling in magick and moonlight.

'I can reach her,' said the baroness, and my knees weakened in sheer relief. 'But you must assist me.'

STONES DREAM. DID YOU know that? So does loam. Leaves and tumbling river-water, flowers and vines and trees—above all, trees. Everything dreams, after its own fashion.

I dreamed with it, for a time; a pebble in rich earth, a droplet of water in a downpour of rain.

Then came a sharp, fierce pain, and a bludgeoning force struck me: once, twice. Thrice.

Something grabbed me—hooked long, relentless fingers into every part of me, and, merciless, *pulled.*

I came forth out of the land in screaming protest, ablaze with searing agony—and then I was free, and whole, and separate, and the pain stopped as suddenly as it had begun.

I lay in a boneless, gasping heap on a very cold floor, blinking in blurry confusion at three figures looming out of the shadows.

Baroness Tremayne, straight-backed, resplendent in her wide-skirted gown: the source of the agony. And the reprieve. 'Hi,' I said weakly, and belatedly croaked, 'Thanks.'

'*Ves.*' The second figure grabbed me, then thought better of it, touched me with gentle hands that shook a little. Jay. 'Are you okay? Gods, I thought we'd lost you.' Something was wrong with his voice: there were tears in it.

'I'm all right,' I told him, and said it a couple more times; he didn't seem to be hearing me properly. I patted his shoulder, his hair, trying, with the little energy I possessed, to comfort him.

The third figure thrust itself rather rudely in upon this tender reunion: a familiar shape, with wild auburn hair and the kind of deeply-etched scowl left by three or four decades of near-permanent irritation. 'Cordelia,' my mother demanded. 'What the *bloody hell* did you think you were doing?'

Then, to my utter astonishment, she threw her arms around me, and squeezed me so tightly I couldn't breathe.

18

'It's done,' I said a little later. 'I think. So I suppose you can go home again.'

Mum rolled her eyes in wordless contempt.

'Not that it wasn't amazing of you to come,' I hastened to add. 'Super appreciated.'

'Farringale has been dead for centuries,' she informed me. 'And I don't mean metaphorically dead. I mean *actually dead*. If you think it's going to be easy to drag it into the modern world then you have bats for brains. They are going to need us.'

We were still in the library, though we'd ascended out of the cellar. We found a crowd gathered there, apparently not waiting for us: our appearance came as a surprise.

A welcome one, to Indira and Rob and Zareen. I was hugged again, quite a lot—even by Indira. 'I found Mab,' she said to Jay, who had not left my side. 'She was—busy.'

'Busy.' Jay's brows went up, though he spoke distractedly. I believe he was preoccupied with making sure I didn't fall over, which was no easy task. My legs felt about as sturdy as lightly blanched asparagus.

'There's, um. A new tree.' She waved a hand vaguely. 'Where the griffins were.'

'A new tree? Freshly minted?' said Jay. 'Out of what?'

'Mab's turned into a tree,' I surmised, less surprised by this than I might have been a week ago. I'd rather liked being a tree, myself.

But Indira shook her head. 'Turned someone *else* into a tree. Take a guess.' She was grinning, standing there with a smile of pure mischief on her youthful face and stone dust all over her hair: a vision less like cool, reserved Indira I had never seen.

'It's Fenella,' said Zareen, before I could make any sense out of my sluggish thoughts. 'Rob took the regulator off her, which didn't make her happy. Then she lost the griffins, too. She came back with murder on her mind, but Mab got to her. Just said "no", like that, and "I'm afraid I have run out of patience," and turned her into a tree. She's a willow. Quite pretty, actually.'

'A weeping willow,' Jay mused. 'Appropriate.'

'Miranda came through, then?' I asked. 'With the griffins, I mean.'

'Probably,' said Zareen. 'Somebody did, anyway. Rob and Melissa and that lot intercepted them. They're coming back in now.'

'I also, um,' said Jay, awkwardly. 'Stuck a tracker on Miranda's back when she went past me. Seems she didn't notice.'

I beamed blissfully at the wonderful man that he was. 'You're a wonderful man,' I informed him, and yawned.

'Someone get her Home,' Zareen suggested. 'You need a week of sleep at least, Ves. You look bloody awful.'

'Thanks,' I said, still beaming.

'We're okay to go, soon,' Indira offered. 'Just waiting to make sure the griffins are safe.'

'Well,' Jay interposed. 'That's what *we're* doing. Your Mum's reorganising half the world, by the sounds of it.'

I could hear her, distantly, barking orders in the crisp tone of a woman who expects to be obeyed, instantly and without question. And she was. Her Yllanfalen contingent were marching out of the library again in twos and threes, dispatched on various missions of rehabilitation.

Their Majesties would probably be pleased, on the whole. There was no one like Mum for getting things done. This time next week, she'd have it spick and span and well on the way to habitable.

'Mum,' I said, and repeated it a bit louder when she clearly didn't hear me.

She appeared at my side. 'Ves.'

I blinked at her, momentarily stupefied. 'You called me Ves.'

By way of answer I received a blank stare. 'And?'

'You've never done that before.'

'Did you want to say something? Because I have a lot to do—'

'Right. Um. Surely it's a bit late to be—you know?' I made a hand-wavey gesture, meant to encompass the entirety of everything she and her entourage were doing.

'Yes,' she snapped. 'It's a bit late. It's four hundred years late, to be precise, and if we want to get this kingdom rolling again there's no time to lose.'

'Right,' I said meekly. 'Carry on.'

I mentally resigned the whole problem of my mother to Mandridore. They'd asked for aid, and they had got it.

Mum stalked off, evidently forgetting my entire existence again between one purposeful stride and the next.

Jay's hand stole into mine, a warm, strong clasp that conveyed far more than words. Faith and love. Comfort.

Stability. I carried his hand to my lips and kissed it. 'You know,' I said mistily, 'I really would like to go Home.'

Epilogue

I sat in a chair in Milady's tower. A chair, an actual real chair; House almost never provided those, not when one was young and fit (sort of) and perfectly capable of supporting oneself on one's own two legs.

Which I wasn't, entirely. Magickally speaking, I'd been scrambled like a jug of eggs, and the body objects to that sort of thing.

A week had drifted by since Farringale, and I'd experienced very little of it. I'd spent an unconscionable amount of time tucked up in bed, with a stuffed unicorn under my arm and a stack of cosy romance novels at my elbow. I hadn't spent an entire week at rest since I'd left university.

In that, as Jay so objectionably points out, I'm not so unlike my mother after all.

'Welcome back, Ves,' Milady had said, very kindly, when I'd taken my place in the hot seat.

She *sounded* okay. 'Thanks?' I said, my voice breaking a bit. I was nervous.

There was no sign of Mab, of course. Her ladyship consisted, once again, of a glitter in the air and a voice that came from everywhere at once. To hear her talk, you'd think her identity remained the darkest of secrets, known to none but the privileged few (emphatically not including me).

It was a pretence I could go along with.

'Are you... well?' said Milady, with a most unfamiliar note of uncertainty in her smooth, measured tones.

'Mostly?' I said, a question more than a statement.

'You performed an astonishing feat of magick,' said Milady, rather generously. 'I wouldn't be surprised to learn that you are suffering some lingering effects.'

Lingering effects. Typical Milady understatement. I hadn't been able to walk for three days. I still needed help to make it to the bathroom and back without folding like an ironing board. I kept crying for no reason whatsoever, and I'd flatly refused to be parted from my unicorn cuddly toy. It sat, even now, under my left arm, a soft, fluffy note of comfort in a world I couldn't process anymore.

'I—' I began, and had to pause, take a shuddering breath. 'I'm—dissatisfied with my performance.' I managed to get all the syllables out before I dissolved into tears again.

'And why is that?' said Milady, still calm. Not the blaze of recrimination that I'd expected, but I was beyond the reach of reassurance at that point.

'I—I—*lost* the magick of Merlin,' I sobbed. 'All of it. It's still there in Farringale, down in the earth, and I don't know how to—get it—back—'

Words failed me after that. Ophelia had been kind about it, on the whole, when I'd told her, but there had been in her face a look of such shock, such utter devastation…honestly, in future I'd rather have to admit to someone that I'd run over their beloved puppy. Or husband.

Milady waited in polite silence while I snivelled, mopped at my nose with a tissue, and—with a few inelegant, gulping breaths—contrived to pull myself together.

Then she said: 'Ves. Why do you think Merlin's magick still exists?'

I groped, frantically, for a vaguely intelligent answer, and came up with nothing. 'I don't know?'

The air sparkled: amusement, perhaps? 'It is not merely for longevity's sake. Those who commit their arts to the care of others—to the future—do so out of love. For magick, and all that magick can do. So. What did you do with this magick that was once Merlin's?

'You saved a kingdom. And not just any kingdom: one of the foremast magickal Enclaves in the country. Farringale will thrive, and it's down, in large part, to you.

'And it's more than just that. You've proved that it *can* be done. In future, many more Farringales and Silvessens will be revived, and thrive. The decline of magick is over, Ves. That is the gift you've given to Britain—to the world—and I hope you will take pride in it, in time.'

I was crying too hard to reply. Honestly, it's embarrassing. I haven't cried half this much since I was six years old. Saving magickal kingdoms reverts a person to childhood, apparently. 'Great?' I managed, choking on a fresh wave of tears.

'Their Majesties of Mandridore couldn't be more thrilled,' Milady offered, like a slightly perplexed adult hoping to bribe a sobbing child with a treat. 'And your esteemed mother—well. Let's just say that her unique talents are being put to excellent use.'

I could well imagine. Farringale as a hive of industry, speedily being put back together by my mother's relentless energy and will. Hordes of talented people pulled in from kingdoms and enclaves across the country, united in their desire to drag the ancient troll capital out of the dustbin of history and into the glittering present.

Their Excellent Majesties, King Naldran and Queen Ysurra, had thus far expressed their appreciation for my efforts by way of gigantic bouquets of flowers displayed in every room I was likely to appear in (no fewer than six presently adorned my boudoir). I had received a personal letter of thanks, signed by both, and a vague but firm promise of nameless rewards to be bestowed in the future—I needed only ask.

And I appreciated it all, honestly. But whenever I thought about it, I couldn't help but see Ophelia's face, white with shock; her fumbling, devastated attempts to be nice about my casual sacrifice of the oldest magick in England.

Not that I had meant to. I hadn't known what I was doing—which was typical of me, wasn't it? Half-crazy Ves, winging it every step of the way. Well, once in a while the results were more devastating than I could ever imagine.

And—more marvellous.

'Ves,' said Milady, sensitive, as always, to some intangible sign of my turmoil. 'I knew Merlin. And I think—I *know*—he would be proud of what you've done.'

I sucked in a shuddering breath, too appalled—and star-struck—to speak, at least for a moment. 'Are you *sure?*' I finally sobbed.

'Entirely. It's what he would have wanted.'

I was going to have a considerable cry about that, it seemed, and *mercy* was I tired of crying. I hoped my shattered nerves would think about recovering themselves pretty soon, or I'd—well, I don't know. Check myself into a peaceful spa resort for the rest of my natural life, probably.

'You made a nice tree,' I said abruptly, apropos of nothing. 'Fenella, I mean. Lovely.'

A pause; then Milady said, 'You are wondering why I didn't do that sooner.'

'A bit.'

She took a while to reply. At length she said: 'It is a question of...hope. That even the most...challenging of us might change, might grow. That I won't *have* to forcibly deprive the Fenellas of this world of action and agency, because they can be trusted to manage themselves.'

I thought about that. Fenella wasn't the only person I'd encountered who'd failed, again and again, to "manage themselves", as Milady put it. 'Do you regret it?' I asked, rather daringly.

'No,' said Milady, but she hesitated as she said it, almost imperceptibly.

'I don't either,' I agreed, with approximately as much certainty.

'Get some rest, Ves,' said Milady, after I'd palpably failed to summon words for a minute or two together. 'There's chocolate in the pot.'

THERE WAS, TOO. IN fact there were three silver pots waiting upon the various desks and tables of my room, each ornately engraved and gently puffing steam. Pup lay curled up on my bed, blissfully asleep, and squeakily snoring.

Jay had awaited me outside the door to Milady's tower-top room, and escorted me back down again once I'd been gently dismissed. He lent me his nice, strong arm, fussed over me flatteringly when I stumbled a bit on the steps, and thanked House very prettily when we found ourselves transported from the bottom of the stairs straight into my room without further difficulty.

Addie had made her personal displeasure with me very blatant indeed. I'd had to recruit Jay, Zareen and Indira to assist me with the steady delivery of freshly-fried chips for her personal delectation, otherwise I'm certain she would never forgive me for almost obliterating myself. It had taken thirty-three portions to date, and we were still trying.

The grove had been still less welcoming. Oh, not that it had rejected me, or anything so impolite. But I could wander about in it on two legs, now; nothing, it seemed, could restore me to my former status as a member of the herd.

Jay gently assisted me back into bed, and tucked my stuffed unicorn toy back under my arm. He was so very obliging as to plant a firm kiss on my forehead, too. He looked deep into my eyes, and said, with conviction, 'You are wonderful, and everything is going to be all right.'

I captured one of his hands, and laced his fingers through mine. 'Have you...' I began.

He waited, and finally prompted, 'Yes?'

'Have you happened to run into Ornelle, lately?'

'No. But I could.'

I dithered on the borders of confession, and finally broke. 'I can't change my hair.'

He glanced, briefly, at the mess of the hair in question, hastily combed with my fingers an hour before, and unchanged in hue since before Farringale. 'That's unaccept-able,' he said.

'I was hoping—I could get my Curiosity back. The ring?'

'I'll get it back,' he promised. 'We can't have you con-fined to a single colour for the rest of your days.'

I wrinkled my nose expressively. 'Or obliged to—*dye* it. Do you know how revolting that stuff smells?'

'I do, yes.'

I raised my brows.

'Sisters,' he explained.

I wondered which of Jay's several sisters had undergone an experimental phase with her hair. Not Indira, anyway. 'You're the best,' I declared sleepily.

Jay stroked my hair. 'I know.'

Tears threatened again, but I was done with resenting them. I'd survived; I was alive, free to drown in the mess of my own emotions if I wanted to. For a while.

And we'd accomplished something nigh on impossible. We'd saved Farringale. Saved magick, rich and old and strange; the future, as far as I could see it, shone.

I opened my arms to Jay, a wordless request—and offer. A plea and a gift: affection, love, proffered and requested. Whatever the future might bring, I couldn't imagine it without Jay beside me.

He didn't hesitate. In another moment he was in my arms, the two of us as close as love could bring us. 'What do you think we should do next?' I murmured against his hair.

He smiled; I could feel the joy surge in him. 'I don't know,' he murmured, 'but it had better be something dazzling. I've developed high standards.'

I thought that over. 'All right,' I agreed. 'Ply me with sufficient hot chocolate, and I can probably muster something at least a little bit dazzling.'

He did; and I did.

But that's a story for another time.

***

Also By Charlotte E. English

Fae Fatales:

Hell and High Water

House of Werth:

Wyrde and Wayward
Wyrde and Wicked
Wyrde and Wild
Wyrde and Wondrous

Castle Chansany:

Volume 1

Volume 2